# with you FOREVER

NASHVILLE STAR SERIES

AVA HUNTER

*With You Forever*
Nashville Star Series, #4.5


ISBN: 978-1-7374743-5-7



Cover Design: Sarah Hansen/Okay Creations
Cover Image: © Regina Wamba
Editing: Eliza Dee of Clio Editing Services
Ebook formatting: Champagne Book Design

## Author's Note

With You Always is, in the end, a story about love and support in hard times. The topic of this novella is something many people have experienced or watched a loved one experience, myself included. It was healing for me to write, and I hope if you've ever needed a story like this, that it's healing for you too. Please note content warnings, but this story does have an HEA, so please be aware of that if you do choose to proceed.

Content Warnings:
-Cancer diagnosis
-Grief
-Anxiety

To every woman who's needed someone to be there, who's ever needed a protector of the highest order, this one's for you.

# chapter ONE

Lacey Sutton hums a tune and wipes at the steam fogging the bathroom mirror. Her bright pink engagement ring sparkles in the overhead light. Long strands of golden hair pool around her slender shoulders. She tightens the fuzzy robe around her waist and smiles back at herself. Back at the endless world of possibilities and happiness she's made for herself these last ten months.

Ever since she moved to Nashville, Lacey's kept her promise to herself to live every day to the fullest. She went on tour with Seth. Lived on a bus for six weeks with Sal and the Brothers Kincaid. Took a breath and took a risk and opened up her own event planning agency, Love Lacey Events.

It was terrifying taking the leap to go solo, but she's worked her butt off. She used all the money she had in savings and took out loans for a minuscule office space in East Nashville. And with Colin Cane still one of her elite clients and Seth talking her up in his music industry circles, Lacey's slowly made a name for herself around Music City.

Back in LA, she never would have taken this type of risk. Fear and doubt would have ruled. But not here. Not with all she's gone through this last year. Not with the strength she discovered inside herself. And especially not with Seth by her side. Always right by her side, singing her praises, helping her out. Bolstering her with his strength, his belief in her.

Thanks to him, her tightly wound life has been shook up in the best kind of way.

No barking bosses jumping down her throat, no sad apartment with broken locks, no missed vacations.

She has time for a life—her life.

Here, in Nashville, she has it all. An amazing sister, devoted friends, a wonderful job, and soon—her dream wedding to her forever soulmate. She doesn't know how she got this lucky.

Lacey fingers the gold locket at her throat. Would her mom be proud of her? The thought flips her stomach over. She hopes so. One thing she knows for sure, she would love Seth.

Eyes misty, Lacey adjusts the towel and exits the bathroom.

Clothes. She needs clothes. She needs to get her to-do list in order.

She needs to plan a wedding.

Now that the tour and Vegas are out of the way, Lacey's main priority is putting the finishing touches on her wedding. The *Star*'s dubbed it the party of the century and she happens to agree with them, even though she'd never tell Seth. She knows she's taking forever to plan it, but that's because she wants it perfect. Especially for Seth. Whiskey. Music. Plaid shirts. Family.

Just the kind of things Seth likes.

Besides, the social crime of the highest order would be an event planner having a very unplanned wedding.

No, it has to be perfect.

Starting with the guest list. It's out of control. There's over three hundred people and it needs to be culled before the invitations go out.

Lacey groans and shakes her head, checklists running through her mind. Despite living with her easygoing country singer, she's still type A at heart.

After a quick change into a silk skirt and an off-the-shoulder sweater, she grabs up a stack of wedding magazines, turns, and runs smack-dab into a wall of muscle in the doorway.

"Ugh, you," she says and then looks up into eyes of ocean blue. Seth's dressed in faded blue jeans and the black Henley she loves. With his tousled sandy-blond hair and sparkling blue eyes, Seth looks so damn country, tan and tall, he's got her mouth watering. Instantly, her stomach curls as she inhales his familiar scent, warm wood and black coffee.

Smirking, he stares down at her. "You in a hurry, princess?" he asks, smoothing a broad palm over the curve of her bare shoulder.

"Don't." She waves a finger. "Do not look at me like that."

"Like what?" An arch of a mischievous brow. The look on Seth's handsome face is full of wild desire. A tug on the waistband of her skirt. "Like you look too damn good? Like you're lookin' late for work, Lace?"

She groan-laughs. Rolls her eyes at his all-the-time charm. "Stop." She palms the front of Seth's chest to control herself. "I cannot be late today."

"Why not?" He pulls her closer. "You got another handsome country singer to kiss?"

Her body responds to him the way it always does. With betrayal. With sheer lust. Damn him. Damn Seth Kincaid.

The stack of wedding magazines slaps the floor.

Seth's lips hit hers. Crushing. Soul-quenching. With a whimper, Lacey gives in. Drinks in his sweet kiss. Her tall, handsome country singer that sets her heart on fire. So what if she's late for work?

If she weren't infuriatingly in love with him, not to mention engaged, she'd say her and Seth living together is a very, very bad idea. Just the simple act of saying hello in the morning ends in a frantic make-out session and a trashed apartment.

If this is what they're like engaged, the honeymoon doesn't know what it's in for.

"We gotta get a new place," Seth murmurs against her lips. He grunts as they knock into a bookshelf. Grips her shoulders and spins her around toward the exit.

"Bigger," she agrees, kissing him back, angling her body just so to avoid a collision with an ottoman. Between building her career in Nashville and Seth's Vegas stint, they barely have time to house-hunt, let alone plan a wedding. "So much bigger."

As they stumble their way into the sunlit living room, bypassing Seth's clasped fiddle case, Lacey unbuckles his belt as birdsong sounds through the open window. The cool March breeze sends a chill down her spine.

Seth tugs the neck of her sweater down. Her bra. Lacey gasps at the heat of his mouth on her nipple. Seth touching her shouldn't make her tremble, shouldn't make her heart pound this fierce, but it does. Over and over again, he touches her like it's their first time.

He backs her against the wall. Drags her leg up his thigh. She shifts her hips as Seth's long fingers move up her skirt to slowly drag off her panties, then dip inside of her. Her eyes flutter, and she'd go limp if it weren't for Seth's broad palm bracing her firmly against him. Seth strips out of his jeans and Lacey lets his stiff erection fill the palm of her hand.

Seth groans at her touch. His heartbeat pumps erratically against hers. "Princess, you ain't playin' fair." Angling into her, he kisses the pulse at her throat, biting its beat gently.

"Never," she gasps.

Her mind turns hazy, a puddle of warmth blooming in her belly.

*Seth. Seth. Seth.*

Her heartbeat.

The love of her life.

Seth grins, whispers against her mouth, "My wife."

She arches a haughty brow. "Not yet."

"You are," he drawls. "You already are, and you damn well know it."

His words—reverent, smug, possessive—rocket through her like sunlight.

Lacey's lips sweep the shell of his ear. "Seth. Please." She arches against the wall, her breasts plumping against his chest. "*Please.* I need you," she whispers, and in answer, he swears, haggard and hungry. Her words like a whip. Their calling card of their love for each other.

He's inside of her like quicksilver, fast and hungry. She

whimpers and Seth grunts his appreciation at the way her nails dig into the meat of his shoulder. Lacey closes her eyes as her body goes molten, her legs spreading as Seth buries himself to the hilt inside of her.

"Christ." Her hair fills his fist. A broad palm is dragged up her thigh. "Your body's got me goin' weak, Lace."

"More," she whines. It's all she can say. She arches her hips, clings to him with her arms around his neck. "Harder, Seth. *More.*"

"Holy fuck, princess," Seth grits out, his lean muscles tensing. "You tryin' to kill me?"

She grins. "Maybe."

With a growl, he quickly flips her around. Her palms flatten against the wall, her cheek on the cool wood. And then, his big hands engulfing her waist, he's slamming into her from behind. Perfect sync. Perfect friction as he fucks her hard and fast.

"*Seth,*" she whispers, moving her hips in circles that have him panting.

Their love. Sweaty and aggressive and broken and still so damn soft it takes her breath away.

Seth settles Lacey on his lap as she adjusts the strap of her bra. Leaning forward, he buries his face in her long blond hair, inhaling her lavender and sea salt scent. When he pulls back, all he can do is sit in a daze and stare. His girl. Gorgeous and glowing after two orgasms. Tousled hair, flushed cheeks, slender legs kicked up over his knees.

She's beautiful. So goddamn sexy that for a second Seth can't breathe. His dick twitches, and he has to fight the urge to take her back into the bedroom for round three. Jesus, this girl. She damn near fucks him up on a daily basis. Fucking owns him just with her smile.

But that's Lacey. His hurricane girl. Messing up his life in the best kind of way.

The only way he ever wants it.

A soft, content sigh. "Now I'm really late."

"The world won't end," Seth drawls, kissing her bronze shoulder. "But if it does, it ain't a bad day to do so, I reckon."

Lacey scoffs. She pokes a finger into his chest. "Smooth talk for a guy who's late too."

He knows he is. He's gotta be across town for a film shoot. The Brothers Kincaid are being interviewed about the history of country music for an upcoming documentary, and if he's late, Luke's gonna have a boot up his ass.

"Hell, I know it," he says, running a hand along her slender thigh. "But it was worth it."

At the compliment, a pleased smile twists her lips. "You're the best worst distraction."

She kisses him quick, then she's off his lap and adjusting her skirt. Seth groans, the loss of her like a sucker punch.

"We have to talk." Lacey stares down at him, her pretty brow furrowed. "Really talk, Seth. About the wedding."

Cocking a brow, he adjusts his cuffs. "You mean all about how we're gettin' married tomorrow?"

She scoffs. "Seth. Be serious."

He grins. Lacey's got that haughty-beautiful look on her face that tells him she's exasperated as hell.

Seth pushes to his feet and zips his jeans. "I am serious. Hell, Lace. It's been ten goddamn months." A grumble tears out of him. He hates that it's been almost a year and she's still not his wife. "We should have gotten married in Vegas."

Two months ago, the Brothers Kincaid played a residency in Las Vegas. He means it in a semi-joking way, but if that's what it took to get him and Lacey hitched, he would have done it. Between Vegas and tours and life, it feels like everything in the universe is trying to stop him from marrying Lacey.

Lacey gasps and wrinkles her nose. "I will not be married by a fat Elvis." She keeps going, giving him a small smile. "We have a date at least."

They do. June.

Too damn long.

Stepping closer, she fiddles with a button on his shirt. "I just want it to be perfect, Seth. I want it to be perfect for *you*."

"I know," he says, catching her hand. Lacey's got a heart of gold. Her selflessness still stuns him. "It will be."

Which is part of the reason it's taking so long. Lacey's been planning their wedding like it's a damn Olympic event.

Still, he'd never deny her this. It's her wedding. A wedding she's been looking forward to since she was a little girl. What Lacey wants, she gets. Seth knows that as a wedding planner, she wants this wedding to be one of the best parties around.

Even if it is going to take her fifty damn years to plan it.

"First order of business is the invitations," Lacey says, fixing her hair in the hallway mirror. "We have to get them out soon or we really won't have a wedding."

Seth hisses an unhappy breath. "How many we up to now?"

Lacey wrinkles her nose, hesitates. "I think . . . three hundred."

His jaw drops. "Christ. How in the hell do we know three hundred people?"

"Blame Luke. He's inviting all of Six String."

Seth rolls his eyes. Both Luke and Lacey are gonna have the entire city at his wedding. He wants it small. The people who matter. Not the ones who want to get rich off a photo of Lacey in a fancy dress or talk his ear off about the next album.

A shake of her blond head. "And it's not just the invitations. We have to talk about the music and the food and my dresses," Lacey rattles off, ticking a checklist on her fingers.

"Listen, I got it handled," Seth drawls. "Invites—email them."

Offended, Lacey scoffs. "Ridiculous."

Seth goes on. "Music—I know a guy. And dresses? As in plural?"

Frowning, she props her hands on her trim waist. "I can't pick one wedding outfit, Seth."

"What about my suit?"

"Like anyone is going to be looking at you anyway."

He barks a laugh.

"And what about the food?" she asks.

"Pizza buffet?"

Her lips flattening, Lacey's hands move to her hips. "I'm gonna push you into a ditch, Seth."

"We'll talk, princess. I promise."

His words soften her face and Seth exhales a relieved breath. He likes to tease Lacey, but making her sad isn't even an option. This wedding is the first step in their married life together. Their future. Their forever. Christ, he craves it. He wants her ring on *his* hand, wants to show the world he's hers. And she's his. If he can help her plan it, take some stress off her shoulders and make a few decisions, then maybe they can get this show on the road.

Seth follows as Lacey moves to the kitchen island to stack wedding magazines and a binder in her oversized purse. His heart clenches as he catches her pretty profile. Pride flares inside Seth. Between his tour and the residency in Vegas, Lacey's been working her ass off to prove to him, to Nashville, that she has what it takes to make it in her career. And she will. She already has.

"Meet for lunch?" he asks, crossing his arms and leaning against the wall. "We can talk about whatever you want."

"Can't," she says, brushing a strand of long hair from her face and locking her eyes with his. "I'm helping Alabama finish planning her housewarming party and then I have a hot date with Sal at the hospital."

It's like having the wind knocked out of him.

Seth frowns. "What's goin' on?" Worry tugs at his heart and he reaches up to rub at his chest. He doesn't remember Luke saying anything about Sal being sick.

"Checkups." Biting her lip, Lacey makes a sheepish face. "I've been bad since I've been back here. Between trying to find a doctor and the tours, I missed my annual mammogram. Sal finally talked me into going with her to get dual exams." Lacey smirks. "I told you last week, remember?" She adjusts the purse on her shoulder, checks the time on her phone. "Which is why now I really can't be late."

Seth shakes his head and swears, angry at himself for forgetting. That's why she couldn't be late today. And here he is, the horny bastard who just uprooted her entire schedule for the day.

"Shit. Lace," Seth says, tearing a hand through his hair. "I'm—"

"Busy." She cuts off his apology with an understanding smile. "We're both busy. It's okay. I get it."

But he shouldn't be busy.

He should never, ever be too fucking busy for her.

Lacey's gaze narrows and she extends a finger, poking it into Seth's chest. "Tonight. You. Me. We talk wedding plans." She lifts her chin, fire flashing in her green eyes. "We actually plan something, Seth. Not kiss."

"But I like kissin' you."

When she groan-laughs, he tugs her to him, not wanting to let her go. Staring into her face, he smooths a hand down her shoulder. "Meet me for a drink at Tonk's and we'll do it, princess."

Approval shines in her eyes. "Save me some whiskey."

Then with one last kiss and a haughty eyebrow raise, Lacey sails past him.

Seth grins, his heart damn near following her out the door.

*His wife.*

He feels like the luckiest son of a bitch in the world.

# chapter TWO

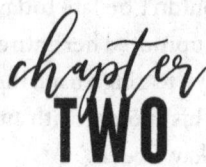

Tonk's is bustling by four in the afternoon. The off-Broadway bar spits neon and beers on draft. Alan Jackson croons from a sputtering jukebox. Peanuts cover the hardwood floor. Even as downright divey as the bar is, Seth considers the bar his and Lacey's. The scene of the crime where he fell head over boots for his ice princess. The bar where they schemed to take down Mort. Where he poured one out last year when he thought he and Lacey were done.

Heavy bootsteps carry across the room as Luke and Seth claim their signature spots at the bar. No one comes forward to disturb them, no one asks for an autograph. Tonk's a safe haven from fans and the likes of the *Nashville Star*.

Luke sighs as the beers are set down. Seth frowns, his gaze narrowing. His brother's been grim the entire afternoon.

"You're thinkin' too much," Seth says as Luke checks his phone for about the eighth time today. His brother's worrying about Sal. It's classic Luke. A goner over Sal and she ain't even in the room.

Luke exhales. "I hate this. Every fuckin' year . . ." He trails off, drowning the rest of his sentence with a long sip of his beer.

Seth hates it too.

Ever since Sal and Lacey's mother died from breast cancer at the early age of thirty-eight, the girls have been diligent with their health and checkups. It also has his brother in knots whenever Sal goes to the doctor.

It's got Seth in knots too.

Jesus, he still feels like an asshole he forgot about Lacey's doctor appointment, now Luke's driving him to drink. Still, Seth tells himself it's routine. It's every year. They'll be okay.

"You ain't drinkin' enough." With a lift of his hand, Seth orders Luke another beer. "We both ain't." He claps his brother on the shoulder giving him a reassuring squeeze.

Luke grunts, his dark eyes faraway.

"Think I'll stop by and see the kid tonight if it ain't too late," Seth says, wanting to take his brother's mind off his worries.

At the mention of his fourteen-month-old son, Cash, Luke breaks into a broad grin. "Nah. He'll be up. He'd love to see you."

Though Seth sees his nephew every Sunday supper, any chance he gets to see him, he'll take it. He loves that kid. Cash is the best combination of all of them—steady and stoic, wild and rebellious. Seth can't wait until the kid is older so he can tell him about all the shit him and Luke got up to as kids.

Damn right he'll be the best bad influence on his nephew.

The clatter of the beer can chimes over the door has Luke twisting on his barstool.

"Everything okay?" he asks as a flustered-looking Jace hustles in, cell phone in hand.

"Emmy Lou's on a tear." Jace chuckles, perching on a stool. "Think she's cooked everything in the damn house by now." He looks down the bar at Seth. "Y'all need a casserole? Or ten?"

"You're gonna need a new fridge." Luke laughs. "You still got five months to go."

Jace rubs his face, signaling for a beer. "Tell me about it."

Seth snickers, taking the opportunity to rib his friend. "Shit, you can't handle one woman. How you gonna handle two more?"

It was only recently that Jace and Emmy Lou found out they were having twin girls. He and Luke had never seen their friend look so shellshocked. Not to mention goddamn ecstatic.

They all are.

Adding two more to their country music family has Seth seeing how goddamn good this life of his is. How damn proud he is that the Brothers Kincaid are living out the songs they write. Women. Whiskey. Family. Friends. Now babies. It'd blow Seth's mind if he wasn't right there with Jace and Luke. In love and sinking.

Jace smirks. "You want to place bets on which one will happen first? Your wedding or the twins?"

Seth scowls. Asshole.

Jace swigs down his beer, glances at Seth. "Could always do what we did and go down to city hall."

Luke laughs, long and loud.

Two months ago, Emmy Lou and Jace found out they were divorced and rustled up a quick wedding courtesy of Lacey that had everyone celebrating long and loud into the night.

Seth shakes his head. "It'd be damn near suicidal telling Lacey to skip the weddin' and go straight to the courthouse. Hell, she'd end my life with just a high heel."

"It's you, Lacey, and a wedding," Luke says. "You ain't got no chance."

"I just want to marry her, and damn fast too," Seth grumbles.

Jace grins. "Y'all got lots of time."

"Yeah."

Seth's throat constricts. He already knows he'll be a mess when he sees her. His wife. Walking down that aisle to him.

Two beers later, a gruff growl signals the arrival of Griff Greyson. The stocky country singer runs a broad palm down his scruffy beard as he sits beside Jace, leaning down the bar to look at Seth. "Saw your girl today."

Seth straightens up at the mention of Lacey. "How'd it go?"

"Spendin' too much money." Griff grins, accepting the beer the bartender slides him. "And that's alright. Alabama gets what she wants. I just sit back and watch." He shrugs. "They got whiskey on the menu, so I ain't complainin'. California does it right."

Seth laughs, pride warming his chest. "Yeah. That's Lacey."

"When's the party?" Jace asks.

"'Bout three weeks." Griff's tawny eyes look them over, his tattooed hands lifting a beer. "Y'all better be ready to get rowdy."

A chorus of agreement and beers are raised.

If someone had told Seth three years ago that the Brothers Kincaid and their families would be close as kin with Griff Greyson and Alabama Forester, he'd have called bullshit. But that was then and this is now, and he's damn proud to consider them family.

For a few long minutes there's the quiet chaos of the bar and the jukebox switching over to Hank Williams Jr.

"Hoo boy," Jace exhales and nods at the television hanging crooked above the bar.

Griff shakes his head, disgust on his face. "Who's the *Star* got its fangs into now?"

In silence, they watch the tabloid news show skewer some newbie country singer, picking apart his past secrets like a bunch of vultures.

"Poor bastard," Jace says, and the men stare at the TV for a long second.

Luke chuckles, but there's no humor in it. "How 'bout you invite 'em to the weddin', Seth?"

Seth rolls his eyes.

That's when Luke leans over the bar, grabs the remote and changes the channel.

A round of applause sounds in the bar.

The music kicks up. Skynyrd. The men's conversation drifts from their girls to their lives. Luke leans into Seth. "How's the house hunt goin'?"

Seth smirks, thinking of earlier today. He and Lacey

bumbling around like two fools in love. Two fools with a goddamn space problem, that's for sure.

"Ain't even started." Seth smears a hand down his face, facing his brother fully. "We need a new place."

"I got a piece of land," Luke says, even-voiced. "You want it?"

Seth does a double take. "You ain't serious."

"Damn serious." A smile cracks Luke's face. "I got a fifteen-acre lot sittin' a few miles from us. Ain't sure if you've thought about buildin' but . . ."

Seth knows exactly what plot of land Luke's talking about. Killer views in all directions, the property's located up on a hill with a small rough road that drops from the hill to the river.

"Sal and I talked," Luke says in a low voice. "Weddin' gift."

Seth arches a brow. "Goddamn big gift."

"You're my brother. My family." Seriousness clouds Luke's expression. "Best gift I can give you. Hell, you livin' next to me and Sal, to Cash, best gift you can give *me*."

His chest tightening painfully, Seth sits there, choked up. The knot in his throat won't let him loose. Boatloads of gratefulness consume him. His brother understands him like no one else in his family. It's always been him and Luke. Since kids, Luke's always had his back and he still has it. He wouldn't be here today if it weren't for his brother and Sal.

The thought of living next to his brother, his best friend, his nephew . . .

Tugging a hand through his hair, Seth shakes his head. "Fuck, man. I don't know what to say."

Luke chuckles. "Say yes."

An excitement he's never known fills Seth up inside. Building Lacey her dream home, giving his girl a closet as big as Montana, giving her everything she deserves and then some. . .

Fuck.

He wants it. With every breath in his body.

"I gotta talk to Lace first, but if she's good . . . yes." Seth grins at his brother. "Fuck yes."

In response, Luke lets out a jubilant whoop, pounds the bar top.

Seth can't wait to show Lacey.

Their future.

Lacey sits next to her older sister on a hard gray chair in the hospital breast center clinic. Her leg bounces a mile a minute as her eyes scour her surroundings. The office waiting room could use some color. It's bland. Depressing. Quiet. Too quiet. Everything she doesn't want right now. She doesn't want to think about what she's doing here. Has never liked these reminders of her mother and her own mortality.

So she resets her thoughts. Turns her mind to prettier things. Like wedding dresses. Her wedding dresses.

She drops her eyes to the folder on her lap. Her wedding planner, where she's torn pages from wedding magazines and curated her magical June wedding. A combination of modern cowboy vibes. The old schoolhouse where they'll marry. Custom cocktails. Eclectic table settings. Wildflowers plucked from Wild Antler Farm. Vibrant colors of lavender, rust, blush, and sand. A bohemian-styled altar. Mini whiskey bottles that double as escort cards and party favors for guests.

She'll never admit it to Seth, but the wedding is out of control.

Only slightly.

Lacey's heart speeds up when she flips to the page containing her wedding dress. Her actual *actual* wedding dress. Sure, she has a pre-wedding dress and a reception dress, but *this* dress—what she'll wear walking down the aisle to meet Seth—is the most special. With a long scalloped train and low V-back and a bow, she can't wait for Seth to see her in it.

Saying their vows . . . taking his last name . . .

Romantic ideas, sure, but Lacey can't help but be a romantic. Especially with Seth. With this man who's loved her better than anyone ever has.

Turning to Sal, Lacey flips the page and drills a nail into the photo of her second dress. "So this one is the reception dress. A mini dress with ostrich-feather cuffs. This one really says I'm going with drama instead of comfort." She glances over. Her sister's not listening. Sal's pretty face is taut with worry as she sits silent and contemplative while Lacey's been rambling a mile a minute.

"Sal?" Gently, she bumps her shoulder into her sister's.

Blinking, Sal looks up and over.

"You're nervous," Lacey says.

Sal looks at Lacey's bouncing leg and smiles. "You're nervous too."

"I know. I just hate this." She draws out her sigh. "Had to drag me along, didn't you?"

Sal laughs, then gives her a stern big-sister look. "You're overdue, Lace. I may have memory issues, but I remember this."

Lacey flinches at the kind admonishment only Sal can dish up. She's had annual mammograms since she was twenty-five. There's no excuse for skipping her checkup, even though she has all the excuses in the book. Moving. Waiting on insurance. Finding a new doctor. Touring with Seth. She put it off too long until Sal booked them both appointments.

Sal adjusts herself in the seat, crossing her arms across her slender frame. "Well, if it makes you feel any better, I hate it too. I can't remember Mom, and yet here I am, going through what she went through." She swallows. "Especially with Cash and Luke . . ."

A pang of pain hits Lacey. Sal's fear is losing anyone in her family—especially Cash. The little baby is the greatest treasure of her life and, if Lacey's honest, everyone else's.

She couldn't imagine not living near her nephew. She's loved these last ten months in Nashville. Making friends, being present, having a family. Being able to see her sister, Cash, whenever she wants has been the best kind of dream.

"Anyway, enough with the sad talk," Sal says with a smile, tucking a long strand of chocolate-brown hair behind her ear. "You were saying about dresses?"

Lacey perks up and flips to the page that contains Sal's rose-colored maid-of-honor dress. But before she can inhale a breath and let her mouth go into overdrive, the door to the exam room swings open.

Lacey and Sal look up.

"Ms. Kincaid?" A nurse stands there with a chart and a smile.

Sal stands. "That's me." She grins at Lacey. "For now."

Lacey squeezes Sal's hand, then watches her disappear into the back room. Nerves bubble for her sister and she says a quick prayer that Sal's okay.

An hour later, Sal slips into Lacey's room. "How'd it go? Was getting felt up wonderful as usual?"

Lacey laughs and adjusts the shoulders of her sweater. "Oh, I loved it. How about you?"

Sal beams, her green eyes bright with relief. "All clear. All good."

Lacey squeals. "We should celebrate. Come to Tonk's with me. Seth and I need to pare down the guest list, and you'll be the perfect one to wrangle Luke." Flicking her hair over her shoulder, she grabs up her purse, then sags back against the wall and wrinkles her nose, trying to chase away her nerves. "That is if I ever get out of here."

She's antsy. All she wants to do is take her planner and go meet Seth.

Sal's eyes widen. "You've been waiting an hour, Lace. That's bullshit," she says, sounding concerned. "I'll go find Mayr."

Lacey hides a smirk. Her big sister practically runs the hospital. Everyone knows and loves Sal.

At the exact moment Sal turns around, the door opens. Dr. Mayr, a man in his early forties, stands there, his shock of bright white hair a contrast to his youthful face. His dark blue eyes warm when he sees Sal. "Sal, good to see you."

"You too," Sal says. "Do you have my sister's results?"

"I do." Mayr adjusts a folder in his hands. His gaze moves from Sal to Lacey. "I was wondering if I could speak with you in private, Lacey."

Instantly, the levity, the warmth, is sucked from the room.

Startled, Lacey looks to Sal, who's gone pale. "What—" Lacey falters. Recovers. "You can tell me with Sal here." When Mayr hesitates, Lacey lifts her chin. "She's my sister. She stays."

"Of course." Dr. Mayr moves to the workstation and click-clacks the keyboard.

Sal's hand snaps out and grabs Lacey's.

After a few seconds, an image is called up onto the screen. Lacey blinks at the image of her breast, suddenly very aware that Sal's grip has turned tight and torturous.

Mayr gestures at the screen. A pencil-eraser-sized spot. "There's a small shadow here, Lacey, do you see it?"

Lacey licks her lips. "Yes." She looks at the doctor. Her heart thumps wildly. "What does that mean? Is it bad?"

"We'd call this an abnormal scan. This shadow here could be nothing. Or it could also indicate the presence of—"

"Cancer," Lacey whispers, a scream freezing in her throat. A numb kind of feeling settles over her.

Sal winces. "Stop," she shushes. But her face has lost all color, except for the bright green blaze of her eyes.

*This is not happening. This is absolutely not happening.*

Lacey shakes her head, feeling like the rug's been pulled out from under her. "I don't understand, I never felt a lump." She fumbles for the words, stumbles around the hot rush of panic and guilt. "I did exams at home, maybe not all the time, maybe not as good as I should have but, but . . ."

"I know this is scary." Dr. Mayr sits on the high chair. "We can't be sure what it is without a biopsy."

Lacey swallows. "Okay."

She and Sal exchange looks of worry.

"We can make an appointment for next—"

"No," Sal interrupts, her gaze hard and determined as she meets Mayr's eyes. Her posture ramrod stiff. "We do it today. I don't want my sister to wait."

Lacey does a double take. Her big sister sounds so fierce she half expects Sal to take off her earrings and start pulling up her hair.

After a beat, Mayr nods. "I'll set something up in radiology. It might be a few hours' wait, but we'll squeeze it in today."

Sal nods, visibly relaxing. "Thank you."

As soon as Dr. Mayr exits the room, Lacey looks at her sister. "Sal."

"I know," Sal breathes, a hand to her heart.

But she doesn't know. Can't know what Lacey is feeling right now. Pure dread.

A wave of loneliness, one she hasn't felt since LA, since she lived with Vivian, crashes over her.

Blinking back tears, Lacey squeezes her sister's hand. Before she can allow herself to be scared, she says, "I want Seth."

She needs him.

Now.

"Joe Turner."

"Cut."

Luke sighs. "Seth."

"Hell no," Seth grumbles, staring into the last dregs of his beer. Griff and Jace have long since gone home and it's just him and Luke, waiting on the girls to get here. "Luke, I swear to Christ, we ain't invitin' Dad's old huntin' buddy. I mean, we last saw the guy, what, twenty years ago?"

Seth frowns down at the list he has on his phone. Hell, if Lacey ain't here yet, then the least he can do is work on the guest list. Trimming the hell out of it, that is. "And take off Mason Vick because that bastard gave us three stars on our last album."

He squints at the names. Ain't that hard to figure out who to cut. Rich execs in suits Seth's barely said hello to at an event, let alone at his own damn wedding.

Luke drags a tan hand through his hair. "We invite Bobby, we have to invite all of Six String."

"Yeah, I know it," Seth drawls. "Fine with me. I really just want to see the guy do the drunken cha-cha."

Luke chuckles. "Don't know how you roped me into this."

"Roped you into it because it's half your damn list, man."

Luke's phone buzzes.

Seth grins at the relief on Luke's face as he brings the phone to his ear.

"Hey, darlin'," Luke drawls. "How's it goin'? Everything okay?"

On his own phone, Seth unlocks his screen, preparing to send a text to Lacey when there's a sharp intake of breath from Luke. Seth looks over.

His brother's face has gone serious. His knuckles wrapped white around his phone. Grooves furrow his brow.

Seth's stomach drops.

*Fuck no.*

Not Luke and Sal. His brother and sister-in-law have had their fair share of heartache the last few years. Fate's gotta cut 'em a fucking break. Just once, Christ, please.

Seth sits quiet, tense as Luke and Sal talk. His brother's voice is hushed and concerned in the low rumble of the bar. Then, Luke ends the call, saying, "We'll be right there."

Seth swallows. "Sal okay?"

Luke hangs his head a moment, a muscle working in his jaw. Then, slowly, he nods. "She is."

A beat. Then—

"Seth," Luke says slowly, his face a worrisome shade of pale. "We need to go to the hospital."

"What?" Seth grabs his brother's arm as Luke slides off the stool. Now it's his panic that's building. "What the hell are you talkin' about? What is it?"

That's when Luke says the worst words Seth's ever heard. Words that cause Seth's heart to flatline. "Seth. It's Lacey."

# chapter THREE

THE TICK OF THE CLOCK MATCHES THE TICK OF LACEY'S heart. Slow. Agonizing.

Hands clasped together, she and Sal are settled into a plush office couch. Dr. Mayr sits at his desk. The radiologist, a woman with short black hair who goes by the name Dr. Vee, is perched on a stool. Lacey's mammogram images glow bright on the screen.

It feels like every part of Lacey is spread open and on display. Like she's floating far above her world, watching everything play out.

The radiologist makes a sound. Gestures at the screen. "Should we begin—"

Lacey opens her mouth, wanting to tell them they're waiting for Seth, for the man who is her absolute calm and center, but before she can do that, the door swings open and Seth walks in.

Lacey's heart leaps in her chest.

"Hey," he says, moving straight for her. "Sorry I'm late." He sits beside her, promptly pulling her into his arms. "You okay?" His voice is soft, but his eyes are pained. He looks uncertain but steady. Determined. Determined to be strong for her.

She gives a small nod, simply melting into the warm safety of his body. "I'm okay." She's never been so happy to see him. He's her home in human form.

Sal leans forward, giving Seth a small smile. "We were just getting ready to talk with the radiologist."

He swallows thickly, his eyes flicking briefly to Dr. Vee. "Then let's talk."

Relief fills Lacey. Seth's determined to get answers, to fix. She couldn't love him more.

"This is Seth," she says to Dr. Mayr and the radiologist. "My fiancé."

The radiologist smiles. "Heard you on the radio."

Seth doesn't smile.

"As we were explaining to Lacey," Dr. Mayr says, picking up the conversation, "Lacey's mammogram came back with abnormal results. There's an irregular area, which you can see resembles a shadow. Naturally, that's cause for concern."

"Christ," Seth grits out, looking like he's been stuck in the face.

"It may or may not have the potential to be malignant. It could also be benign. Either way, it is cause for concern, which means in a few minutes we'll do a biopsy under live ultrasound guidance."

A muscle clenches in Seth's jaw. "What's that?"

Dr. Vee speaks up. "It's where we insert a needle into the breast to obtain a tissue sample."

Lacey flinches.

Seth hisses an unhappy breath. "Jesus. You put a needle in her?" He regards Lacey with a pale face, then looks at the radiologist.

"It's standard procedure."

Sal leans in. "It doesn't hurt, Seth."

But it only causes his scowl to deepen.

"How long does that take?" he asks.

"It's easy. Less than an hour." The radiologist smiles at Lacey. "Local anesthesia. You'll leave with a Band-Aid over the incision and instructions to take it easy for the rest of the day."

Sal jumps in, taking over for Seth. "And then what?"

"Then we send Lacey's biopsy to a lab to analyze."

Lacey, bookended by both Sal and Seth, looks between them. She's so damn grateful they're asking questions, taking charge, making the doctors break it down for her like she's a five-year-old, when all she can do is sit stunned. She can't process—she switched off at "potential to be malignant." Like new information about a potentially deadly disease will not compute in her rigid type A brain.

Seth's hand tightens over hers. "She'll be okay, right?" he asks, a knot bobbing in his throat. "She has to—" He breaks off, swallowing his next words.

An icy chill sweeps over her and Lacey closes her eyes.

*Be okay.*

"Let's take it one step at a time, okay?" Mayr says, holding up a hand. "I know it's frustrating and scary not having answers, but we'll get those with the biopsy. Results take about one to two weeks, but then we'll know what we're dealing with."

"Two weeks?" Lacey blurts, her stomach instantly turning. "But that's so . . . so long." She can't handle two weeks. Fourteen days of waiting. Of fearing the unknown.

A shuddery breath rolls out of Lacey and her eyes blur. Seth rubs slow circles on her back, telling her to relax. Trying to stop her from spiraling. From thinking the worst. Because that's what she's always done, isn't it?

She doesn't want to go back there. That dark, lonely, doubtful place she once lived.

"I understand." Mayr's smile is sympathetic. "The wait is a pain. But the good news is, the sooner we do the biopsy, the sooner we get results."

"Are you ready, Lacey?" the radiologist asks.

Sal looks at her, her face a mess of nerves.

No. She's not ready. Not for this. Never for this.

Still, she inhales a steeling breath and, on unsteady legs, stands. Everything will be okay. She can show Seth and Sal that she will be okay. Lifting her arms, she lets them drop to her side. "Let's get this show on the road."

"Can I go with her?" Seth asks, moving to stand with her.

"I'm afraid not. I'm sorry."

Seth makes a miserable sound, his tight grip on her hand not loosening.

Heart aching, Lacey turns into him, resting a palm over his thundering heart. "I'll be okay, okay?"

Seth blows out an unsteady breath. "Okay."

In low tones, Sal and Luke speak in the visitor's lounge. Only Seth tunes out the conversation. He sits in a hard plastic chair, head in his hands, trying to remember the steps to breathe. It's only a needle, a little needle in Lacey, is what Sal told him, but that's not what's got him scared shitless.

It's the spot. The small spot, the size of a pinhead, he saw in the radiology images.

In her body.

Christ. He's never been more terrified in his life.

He's felt fear before. When Luke and Sal were in the plane crash. When Lacey nearly drowned last year. When Cash was born. But this—this is a combination of fear and rage. Some bone-deep need to punch a wall and scream at the same time.

He should be back there with her. All he knows is when he saw Lacey sitting in the doctor's office, looking so vulnerable, so breakable, his blood ran cold.

Seth lifts his face from his hands and breathes out.

With one phone call, his entire life's been sideswiped.

It was only an hour ago that he was waiting on Lacey to have a drink and finalize their wedding plans, and now, he's at the goddamn hospital, needing to see Lacey so bad he aches.

Still, he reminds himself they don't know anything yet.

Because he's Seth Kincaid, his brain wants to dwell on the worst, wants to panic, but he has to focus on Lacey. On being strong for her.

He can do that.

He can be her rock.

"Fuck," he exhales, lifting his face. "How long does it fuckin' take?"

A hand on his shoulder has him turning. Sal. Her lower lip pulled between her bottom teeth.

"It should be soon, okay?"

Boot kicked up on his knee, Luke studies him. "Hang in there, man."

Seth nods, shifting his gaze to the stack of Lacey's wedding magazines beside Sal. The backs of his eyes start to burn. He'd give anything to be talking china patterns right now instead of cancer.

Christ.

Cancer.

He looks at Sal. "What do you think?"

He doesn't need to say anymore. His best friend reads him. Understands his train of thought.

"I don't know." A shaky breath rattles out of her. Luke pulls her close and she closes her eyes. "I just know Lacey. Either she won't take it well or she'll act like everything's fine."

A muscle jerks in his jaw. "I know."

Fake it or break, those are the options with Lacey.

If he's scared, he can't imagine what Lacey's beautiful whirlwind brain is thinking.

His girl. And he knows her. She'll panic, spiral. Then snap.

He's got to be the one to keep her steady.

Sal turns into him, clutches his hands. Hers are cold, shaky. "Don't let her read articles."

Seth snorts. "I like how you think I got a choice in the matter."

Her lips thin.

"This is Lacey we're talking about here."

Sal's shoulders sag. Fresh tears leap into her eyes. "I know."

A brick forms in his throat. "I'll make sure she's okay, Sal. I swear it."

Always. It's his lifeblood. Protecting Lacey. She's his. Nothing will touch her. Absolutely fucking not.

Luke's drawl is quiet. "We'll get her there. Whatever you two need, you got it."

As Seth meets his brother's dark brown eyes, understanding and pain passing between them, he sees something else. Fear.

Fear that if this all goes south, Luke loses Sal and Seth both.

Silence falls.

A sharp intake of air has Sal sitting up straight in her chair. Seth's eyes sweep to her, then the spot where her gaze is lasered.

Dr. Mayr appears in the hallway. "We're all done," he says, scanning their group. "We should have the results in seven to ten days."

"That's too damn long," Seth rumbles. His fingers flex. The dark urge to hit something, someone, crashing over him like a tidal wave.

Sal grunts softly, as if she agrees.

"How's Lacey?" Luke asks, but his eyes are on Seth.

"She's in recovery." Dr. Mayr gestures at the hallway. "She's resting, but she should be good to head home." He inclines his head toward Sal, then Seth, hesitating. "I can take one of you to her room."

With that, Seth stands, steadies his heart and his hands, and follows the doctor down the hall. He can feel Sal's eyes on him. He knows she'd give anything to be with her sister, but he's a selfish bastard.

He has to see her first.

Inside the room, Lacey sits on the edge of the bed, already dressed, the back of her left hand wrapped in a bulky bandage.

Seth's heart squeezes at the sight of his feisty hurricane girl. She looks so fragile surrounded by machines and tubes and wires, all he wants to do is pick her up in his arms and rush her out of her. He wants her out of the hospital.

He doesn't want this place to fucking touch her.

Safe and warm and in his arms.

That's where she's going.

"Hey, princess," Seth says, shutting the door behind him.

"Hi," Lacey says, turning weary sedative-laced eyes toward him. Her beautiful face is pale; her long blond hair hangs over her shoulders.

"You ready to go?" He edges toward her. She looks like she's on the verge of falling over.

Relief sweeps across her face. "Yeah. I am."

She stands, teetering in her heels. Seth pulls her against his chest, holding her tight. She wraps her arms around his waist and leans against him. It's all he wants to do. Hold her. Keep her safe. Keep her close.

So damn close.

He brushes back her hair, kisses her cheek carefully. She smells like harsh chemicals and antiseptic, but Seth doesn't care. She's never been more beautiful. Tears fill his eyes as he kisses the curve of her neck.

Mouth pressed to his ear, Lacey grips the front of his shirt, her voice a broken whisper. "Take me home, Seth."

# chapter FOUR

Seth flips on the apartment light and Lacey slings her heavy bag on the table, the stack of wedding magazines slipping out to lay accordion style on the long kitchen table. At the sight of them, she turns away. All she wanted hours earlier was to talk cake, talk invites, and now here she is.

Her life suddenly firebombed.

A heavy silence fills the apartment. Seth moves quietly around her, locking the door, setting bags of fast food on the counter since no one was in the mood to cook. Mundane tasks that have her feeling like she's jumping out of her skin.

Tonight feels too big. Like her brain hasn't yet caught up with the news.

Because what does she do now? Go on, pretend her life is just perfectly fine while she waits on test results that could make or break her? When she could be walking around with cancer in her body? When she could end up dying like her mother?

Her mind tries to make sense of it, is swamped with more questions than answers. Has she been feeling off? What if she'd never gone in? What if she'd gone in sooner? What if—

*No.*

*Stop.*

She needs to stop thinking like this. She's a pro at torturing herself. At thinking the worst. At taking things on all on her own. Once upon a time, she'd snap like a twig. But she's grown. She's better at believing in herself, at taking risks, at being gentle with herself, especially with Seth and her family around, but tonight, the negative thoughts want to rear their ugly head.

She'll never be able to relax now. Not with this hanging over her head. Not until she knows her results.

The small bandage on her breast itches and she closes her eyes against the foreign sensation.

She resets.

Breathes.

Focuses on what she loves.

Who.

*Seth.*

"What do you think, princess?" Seth's deep drawl floats somewhere behind her. "Let's get some food in you, then get you to bed. I want you re—"

He never gets the chance to finish his sentence. Lacey slams him back against the front door and crushes her lips to his. Kisses him with unyielding force, with an almost frenzied need to chase away the last several hours.

To forget.

With a groan, Seth grips her shoulders, pulling her close. She hugs him, anchoring herself. Melting into his strength. His hands go to her hair and Lacey arches her body against him. Slips a lean leg around his thigh.

The kiss turns insistent, frantic.

Until Seth breaks it.

"Lace," he gasps, lust and concern warring in his eyes. "We can't. You gotta rest, princess."

She shakes her head. The worst words he could say. Her body is screaming at him for him to take her hard and fuck her senseless. "Please. You'll be careful with me, won't you?"

He nods, his throat bobbing hard. He stares at her with a pale face. Love and sorrow in his eyes. "Always."

She tilts her chin up. "Then please, Seth. I need you." Her fingers curl into the fabric of his shirt. "I need this."

When he hesitates, Lacey drops her hand, cupping the

silhouette of his dick through his jeans, causing Seth to grit out a curse. "Please." She nips at his throat. Trembles against him. "Treat me rough."

He closes his eyes. "Lacey. I can't hurt you."

"You won't. You *won't.* I trust you," she whispers, already unzipping his jeans.

For one night, she's going back. Back to their bad habit. *Her* bad habit. She wants the release, wants to feel alive, wants to feel strong. Wants rough, hard, sweaty sex that made her forget her pain, made her forget everything bad in her life and replaced it with the good.

Today has her feeling out of control. And this is the one bad habit she can go back to when she gets this way. Nothing else.

*Seth.*

Seth groans as she wraps her hand down the hard length of his cock and pumps. "Princess . . ."

She lifts her chin, aching for him to fuck her. "I need to know I won't break."

At that, his eyes flash. "The hell you're breakin'. I won't let you."

Strong arms hook around her waist.

Seth's mouth crashes into hers.

The wedding magazines hit the floor.

Lacey's slammed onto the edge of the table, her skirt shoved up around her hips. She wiggles as Seth advances, pinning her arms above her head, stretching her out long and lean as he dives back into her lips. Lacey mewls at the heat of his lips, arching against him. She throbs down below and when she presses her hot center against him, Seth moans. He's just as turned on, hard as steel, his erection straining against her thigh.

Every inch of her is sensitive, on edge.

Seth reads her. Reads what she wants. Aggression.

Tugging on her hips, removing her panties, he scoots her an inch closer to the edge of the table. His breaths are hot and searing on the inside of her legs and then she lets out a gasp. Seth eats her like it's his last meal. Like he's a famished man and she's got his order every damn time. Her nails dig into the meat of his muscular shoulders. Seth works his tongue over her clit, faster and faster, until she's swollen and pulsing.

And then she's quaking, dripping down below.

Lacey shudders as Seth licks up the inside of her thighs, sucking her dewy sweetness off her skin. Then he pulls back.

She whines at the loss of contact, only Seth's standing, caging her in his arms.

Dipping down, he breathes hot into her ear. "I'll never fuckin' let you break, Lacey. You hear me, princess?"

The most beautiful words she's ever heard.

She trembles, resisting the urge to shatter.

Slowly, he unbuttons her blouse. She strips him of his shirt. Her breath catches at the sight of Seth's toned body, his muscular arms. So tan and lean and gorgeous, it pushes her past the edge of sanity.

That's when she realizes Seth's staring at her.

The sight of the bandage on her breast has made his face soft all over, has stilled his previously roving hands, but Lacey pushes through it. Pushes him.

"Fuck me," she demands, tilting her chin to lift her face to his. The worry in his eyes dissipates, his lust and love completely off the charts, and Lacey's heart skips several beats.

No one loves her, can love, will ever love her, like Seth.

Tan hands cradle her heaving rib cage, pressing her back down on the table. Seth leans over her, his chiseled form hot against hers. He pants against her throat as he bars a forearm over her clavicles. Lacey wriggles beneath him and then he's inside of her.

Taking command, he thrusts hard, his hips smashing into hers. The table shakes beneath them.

Lacey cries out, her eyes rolling back into her head, as the hard length of him has her opening her thighs wider.

"Lacey," Seth breathes. "*Lacey*. Christ." His long fingers wrap around her wrists, slide up to thread with her fingers. "I love you.

I love you." His drawl is a husky rumble as he repeats the words in her ear.

As Seth drives into her, warmth, that familiar golden glow behind her eyes, builds. And then her pussy's clenching, her mouth popping on an O as she's hit by the orgasm. She lets go and Seth soon follows. The two of them crying out, shuddering, raggedly calling each other's names as the squeaking table slowly quiets.

Lacey lies there dazed.

Relieved.

Quenched.

*Seth.*

Her safety.

Sanctuary.

Love.

It's only when Seth slips out of her and hauls his jeans back up that she feels his absence, the loss of his warmth, and it's like a dam breaks inside of her. A tidal wave of desperation. No more pretending.

When she bursts into tears, she's already in Seth's arms.

Her lithe frame cradled tight against him, Seth carries Lacey down the hall to their bedroom. "Shh," he says, kissing her brow. Her entire body shakes with sobs. "Hold on, princess. I got you."

He's been expecting this. A breakdown. It's about damn time. After years of being friends, and now in love and living together, Seth knows she's taking this hard. Lacey, his Lacey, needed comfort, and now she needs to break.

Still holding her, Seth silently climbs into bed, curling her up in his arms. Tremors ripple through her body as she weeps. Raw, broken sobs fill the room, breaking Seth's heart.

Seth waits, letting her have her worry, her pain. All he can do right now is just be here. Thankful that she's letting him in. That she's not pushing him away.

Seth kisses her, tightening his hold on her waist. Lacey trembles as she buries her face into his neck. She smells like sex and hospital. Seth's eyes flicker. The small bandage on her breast churns his gut, brings him back to reality. That's when he sees them. Imprints, bruises on her thighs from his fingers where he gripped hard.

Fuck.

He's an asshole being so goddamn rough with her after what she went through today. He was incapable of working his mind over what just happened, of having the power to resist. He had a cock as stiff as a tire iron and she was begging him in that pleading voice and he couldn't say no. Never ever can he keep his hands, his heart, off this woman. Still, he knows what she needed—comfort—and it was a way to calm her. To help her.

There are worse bad habits she could have.

Seth will never let her go back there.

Soon, Lacey's trembling body stills. Her breathing goes back to normal. Her sobs ebb. Silence fills the bedroom. Seth holds her, thinking she's asleep when her soft voice says, "This is all my fault. I skipped my appointment. I should've—"

"Shhh. It ain't your fault," he says, adjusting her in his arms to meet her tearstained face. "You did nothin' to cause this, Lace."

"But I did." She wipes her nose with the back of her wrist. Once again, her green eyes fill with silver. "I waited too long, and now it's going to be bad news. Awful."

He strokes her damp cheek. "Princess, you're worryin'. I know you; you're thinkin' the worst. And we ain't doin' that. Not until we get answers."

Easier said than done. Seth's scared shitless. But he's trying. Digging deep for strength for Lacey. Falling apart isn't an option. At least not in front of her.

"Give it to me," Seth whispers softly into her hair. "I can take it, princess."

All her fear, her pain. It's his. She can't do this alone.

He won't let her.

A sniffle. "I'm scared, Seth. What if the results are bad? What if I—"

"Don't," he says, his chest straining.

He closes his eyes, absolutely refusing the rest of her sentence. He thought he could handle it. But he can't.

Not this. Never this.

A heavy silence. Then in the smallest voice he's ever heard, Lacey asks, "What if I die?"

"You ain't gonna die." He clears his throat, trying not to acknowledge how jagged his breathing's become. How his heart is slowly disintegrating in his chest. "I almost lost you once. It ain't happenin' again."

Lacey lies there, still, not speaking.

"We're in this together, you hear me?" He tries to catch her gaze, but her face lolls in his hand. "Lace. Baby." He's desperate for her to look at him; he needs the green of her eyes on his, needs her to understand. Finally, she looks at him wearily, and he cups her cheek in his hand. "If you ain't okay, I ain't okay. And you're gonna be okay, okay?"

Her eyes, dazed from pain and exhaustion, clear. The relief he feels at seeing some of Lacey's old stubbornness, her strength, return is endless.

"Okay," she says, giving a small nod. Looking like she's decided to believe him.

*Christ.* Let him be right.

Leaning back down, Lacey rests her golden head on his chest, strands of her hair tickling his skin. "What do we do now?"

"You sleep," he says, curling her close.

Because he already knows he won't.

# chapter FIVE

THE NEXT MORNING, SETH WAKES TO THE BRIGHT BLAST of March sunlight. He swears. It's too fucking early to be morning. He stayed awake for hours last night, Lacey sleeping on the pillow beside him, his mind a storm of thoughts, irrational, panicked until late into the midnight hour.

With a groan, he stretches his arms out, reaching for Lacey's warm body, but all he finds is an empty bed. He sits up, scanning the room, his heart pounding in his chest.

*Goddamnit*. Where is she? She should be in bed, resting.

"Lacey?" He scrambles out of bed, the beat of his heart unsteady, and he kneads his chest like he can kick it back into the right gear. "Lace?" After checking the bathroom, he rushes into the living room. "Lacey?"

"Seth?" Lacey turns, her green eyes wide and concerned at the way he's blasted into the living room. "What is it?"

Lacey's at the coffeepot, already dressed for the day in a tweed blazer, high-waisted jeans, and a furry pink bandeau top. Her blond hair is pulled back into a sleek ponytail, her beautiful face placid and calm. Like last night never happened. Lacey letting him see her vulnerable ain't happening for more than twelve hours.

But Seth knows better. The dark circles under her eyes tell him she didn't get much sleep either.

He strides toward her, lifting a brow. "You oughta be in bed."

She frowns, her nose wrinkling in that adorable way. "Ugh. Don't be all . . . Seth about this." A shake of her head as she pours him a cup of coffee and slides it his way. "I feel fine. Just a little sore. Besides, the doctor said—"

Crossing his arms, Seth leans back against the cabinets. "The doctor don't clear you. I clear you. And you ain't workin'. Not yet."

She huffs. Her eyes flash in disagreement. "You're overcompensating," she sniffs. "From LA."

He scowls at the reminder. An image of her collapsing in his arms at Colin Cane's party instantly has his heart palpitating hard. Even a year later, he's an overprotective son of a bitch after her mugging. Nothing touches Lacey and he'll damn sure make sure of it.

He takes a step closer to her. "Don't make me put you over my shoulder, princess."

Lacey's lips quirk in amusement. "I have a full day of clients, Seth. I can't just stop." Chin up, she reaches out, palming his cheek. The look on her face—a distraught desperation—has him relenting. She lowers her voice. "I have to work, okay? I have to do normal stuff or I'll go crazy. Please." A tight smile appears on her face. "Besides, like you said, we don't know anything yet."

Protection, pride, twists his heart. He understands. Christ, how can he not? This is Lacey's way of coping. Keeping busy or distracting herself so she doesn't think about the what-ifs. And she should do that. Even if all he wants to do is keep her home and close to him. But he can't be afraid, and he sure as shit can't let on to Lacey that he's afraid.

"Fuck," Seth breathes, taking her hand to draw her into him. He wraps an arm around her neck, kisses her temple. "You're right. I'm sorry. All this, it's just—"

"A lot."

"Yeah."

Then, trying to create some attempt at normalcy, he gives her a crooked grin. "Before you go, what do you say we finally pair down this list and get these invites in the mail?" He spins her wedding planner toward him and opens it to the guest list.

A wary look crosses Lacey's face. "Maybe tonight?"

"We got that gig at the Bluebird. Damn." He tears a hand through his hair. "I'll cancel."

"No. We'll get to it." She grabs her bag, and Seth grabs her arm.

"What about breakfast?"

Her smile, stretched thin, doesn't reach her eyes. "Grabbed a granola bar."

She tries to turn away again, to move, but Seth holds her tight. He searches her face, his stomach a slow roll of worry. "Lace. Don't shut down on me."

She swallows. "I won't. I'm fine, Seth. I'll be fine."

*Fine. Fuck.*

If he hates one word in the English language, it's *fine*.

With one last kiss, Lacey turns on the toe of her high-heeled shoe and struts out the front door.

Blood turning to ice, Seth stares at the left-behind wedding planner. The planner Lacey's never without.

Tilting his head up toward the ceiling, Seth drags a hand down his face.

It's going to be a long two weeks.

Lacey lets out an under-her-breath swear when she pulls into the driveway of Alabama's house. The seat next to her is empty of its usual passenger. Her wedding planner. She left it on the counter when she left Seth.

But does it matter? Planning a wedding? What if—

*Stop.*

Screwing her eyes shut, Lacey lets out a frustrated growl.

No doubt.

Time to compartmentalize. It's what she does best. A coping tactic she hasn't fully used since she left LA. Since her mugging. Shove her emotions into a box, forget about them until they crack and claw and rear their ugly head at the very worst possible time.

Worry about it later. Worry about it when she needs to worry about it.

She allowed herself a slight slip last night, but no more. She has to rally for Seth. She has clients that depend on her. Her career can't take a hit. Her wedding still needs to be planned.

She'll wait to freak out.

She'll wait to break.

It won't be bad news.

It can't.

Seth won't let it, she reminds herself. A stupid notion, she knows he can't control acts of God, but there's some part of her that believes it. Believes he'd fight heaven or hell for her. Believes that the phone call coming her way has nothing but positive and good and healthy news. Last night, he was her protector. He knew exactly how to calm her anxiety, her fears. He took on her pain and made it his. Blue eyes filled with conviction that she'd be okay. It was a reminder to her that, good or bad, angst or adventure, they take it together.

She only hopes it won't be too much for him.

She had woken last night to find him still awake, staring at the ceiling, his handsome face creased in worry.

Seth's strong, but she has to be strong too.

She pulls out her phone and checks it for a message from the clinic, even though she knows it's too early. Wishful thinking.

What she needs today is *not* to be a walking ball of anxiety. Her fingers itch to Google. To hop on WebMD and scare herself to death. To—

"California?"

She jumps at the sound of her nickname. At the hard rap of knuckles and rings on her window.

Blinking her way out of her thoughts, Lacey smiles at the gruff face of Griff Greyson. With a sharp inhale, she sticks her phone in her purse and scrambles out of the car. She groans, seeing her heel stuck in a crack in the driveway. "Damn it," she mutters. She's a hot frazzled mess. Then, she gives her entire body a jerk so hard, she nearly topples over in her haste to get free.

"Easy," Griff says, steadying her by her elbow. His tawny eyes check her over. "You okay?"

She huffs and sweeps a hand down her blazer. A flush of heat on her cheeks. "I'm late."

A chuckle rolls out of him. "Al's inside."

"Thanks," Lacey says and struts toward the stairwell of the old Victorian house. Once an old fixer-upper, it's now a renovator's dream home thanks to Alabama and Griff's handiwork.

Inside, she's greeted by Alabama and a flourish of warm hugs and sweet tea. "Sorry I'm late," Lacey says, setting her bag on the kitchen island. "You ready to put the finishing touches on this party?"

"Lord, am I ever," Alabama drawls, her bright red hair tied up with a blue bandana. "I can't believe it's almost here. Now we get to show it off. All our blood, sweat and tears."

"And style," Lacey adds.

Alabama chuckles. "Think I'm more nervous than goin' on stage."

Lacey laughs at Alabama's excited earnestness. And in that instant, her chest unlocks. This. This is what she can focus on. Parties. Her career. Making people happy. Instantly, her mind feels lighter. Freer.

"Well, don't be nervous. That's my job." She flashes a bright grin. "C'mon. Let's walk."

As the women walk through the space, Lacey detailing where the bar and the temporary dance floor will go, she can't help but marvel at the strange turn their friendship has taken.

It wasn't until last year that their tentative friendship blossomed into something real. Up until then, Lacey had held a grudge about Alabama kissing Luke, what she did to her sister, but when the truth came out, when Sal defended both Griff and Alabama, they slowly connected. It's part of the reason Lacey loves living in Nashville. She has a group of built-in friends, strong, loyal women who have all fought to get where they are, and she couldn't be more thankful to have them in her life.

Alabama and Griff asking her—trusting her—to plan their housewarming party means the world.

Means she can't mess it up.

When they're finished walking the space, they settle at the marble island on big barstools made of mango wood.

On her iPad, Lacey finds Alabama's file, then pulls up the RSVP list. "So now that we're three weeks out, I have most of the RSVPs. Thirty yeses, ten nos. This is the last walkthrough, so speak now or forever hold your peace, and by that, I mean feel free to call me at two in the morning, anytime, to change anything. The day of, the caterers will be in at ten to prep. And I will be here at four. You don't need to worry about anything except having fun."

Alabama stares at her with an expression of awe. "How are you doin' all this and plannin' *your* weddin'?"

"Just like you did all this and a tour." Lacey roves appreciative eyes over Alabama and Griff's adorable home. Soft natural light streams through the floor-to-ceiling windows, the backyard a lush and tranquil space. "I really love the house, Alabama. You've done so much and it shows."

A thoughtful smile tugs at Alabama's lips. "I put a lot of work into this little fixer-upper and found gold." She turns a rueful eye toward Lacey. "Kinda like Griff."

They share a laugh. Alabama, refilling their drinks, asks, "Are you and Seth plannin' to move after the weddin'? I know you're in that apartment on the river."

"I hope so," Lacey says with a smile.

She can't wait to have this with Seth. A house. A home. Her and his style, minus the cramped bathroom quarters.

Then just as the happy thought comes, it's gone.

Why is she thinking about the future?

What future? Does she have a future?

Stop.

Stop.

*Stop.*

"Lacey? Everything okay?" Alabama's soft Texas drawl interrupts her spiraling thoughts.

*I'm fine.*

The lie's on the tip of her tongue. Her ingrained habit. Put on a brave face, pretend everything's fine, pretend like she's not a hot mess of a woman.

But Alabama's soft question and concerned face have her throat in knots. Have her wanting to toss aside that ice-cold chill she's used to channeling and instead open up.

Tears suddenly springing to her eyes, Lacey takes a deep, shuddering breath, then says, "No. I'm not. I went to the doctor yesterday and . . . they found something in my breast." Her voice catches. "I—I had to have a biopsy."

Eyes popping open, Alabama palms her mouth. "Oh Lord, Lacey. I'm so sorry. Can I do anything?"

"No. No one can." Her eyes blur. "What's the saying? Expect the worst, hope for the best? I just have to wait for my results."

"How long?"

"A week. Or two."

Alabama reaches out to squeeze her hand. "I'd be a mess."

Lacey inhales a stubborn breath. "I have a good doctor. I have Seth and Sal."

Alabama nods. "Yeah, you do." She gives a small smile. "You have us too, okay? You call if you or Seth need anything. I mean it. I can cook a mean casserole. And Griff, he can . . . well, he can rant at the world if ya want."

The kind offer fells Lacey and in spite of her nerves, she lets out a sob-laugh. "Thanks. I appreciate it."

"Y'all okay?"

Griff, appearing in the kitchen, splits a concerned look between them.

Turning away to wipe her tears, Lacey closes her iPad. "Just finishing up."

Griff whisks his hands together. "Hell, I'm excited. No more ladders and hammers." He steps close to Alabama, curling his arm around his wife's shoulder. "Just party time."

Alabama smiles up at him. "Betcha I could still get you on a ladder, Greyson."

"Sweetheart, you just tell me the time and place." With a glance at Lacey, he says, "You think we could get a tailgate goin' an hour before the party?"

Her eyes narrow at the request. "That's undignified even for you, Griff."

He barks a laugh, his tawny eyes all mischief.

"It's going to be fabulous," Lacey says, plastering a smile on her face and meaning it. Whiskey and sunshine and fabulous friends. Here and now, she's resolved to take a lesson from Seth—not to worry until she has to.

*Fabulous,* she thinks as she looks out the window. *It'll all be fabulous.*

And so will her test results.

# chapter SIX

TEN DAYS.

Lacey's spent ten torturous glacier-paced days waiting on her results. Each day she's put one foot in front of the other, burying herself in work, in wedding plans, Googling symptoms and then telling Seth to hide her phone, drinking copious amounts of wine with Seth late at night after they tried to fall asleep and failed miserably. Yes, her coping skills are shit, but finally, here she is.

Now, her hands clasped in theirs, Seth and Sal sit beside her on the long tan couch in Dr. Mayr's office. The room's a ticking time bomb of nerves as they wait on the doctor. She can feel Seth's pulse in his palm, his jaw rigid and unmoving.

Lacey steels her spine. She's ready for this. No matter what it is, she needs to know. Her heart, her sanity, needs this.

Reality.

Sal's soft voice sounds. "Good or bad, they never tell results over the phone," she says, leaning forward to look at Seth, her sister doing her damndest to be their ever-steadying calm.

Seth exhales. "Wish I had a goddamn drink right now."

Lacey arches a brow. "Whiskey?"

His face softens with love. "You know it, princess."

The door opens. Closes. Dr. Mayr crosses the floor and settles behind his desk. The doctor's face is unreadable as he clears his throat and says his hellos.

Sal's worried eyes flit to hers. "It'll be okay."

Lacey's heart begins to crash around in her chest.

She knows.

She *knows.*

Lacey stares at Dr. Mayr. "It's cancer," she says before he has a chance to say anything.

Because it's the only way this could work out. She's half her mother and she and Sal rolled the dice to take on her story. Sal's already had her bad shit in life.

Lacey wins this.

Dr. Mayr, his face sympathetic, nods. "It is."

Cancer. A spark goes off in her brain. Setting the fuse, firing every doom cylinder in her mind. Her worst fear. This is how she dies. Like her mother. In pain. Alone.

A choked voice of anguish. "No."

Lacey looks to her left. Seth shakes his bowed head like he can't process the news. His fists sit clenched on the knees of his jeans. Fighting to stay seated, to not explode.

Sal's gone pale except for the fierce flaming of her cheeks.

Dr. Mayr continues. "The thing is you have the best kind of cancer."

Seth lifts his face, growls. "What the fuck does that mean?"

Mayr leans forward. "What you have, Lacey, is stage zero ductile carcinoma in situ. Basically, it means we caught it the earliest we can."

She finds her voice, even as she sits frozen, one hand on her chest to calm her thumping heart. "And that's good?"

"That's great. That means we can treat it before it gets too aggressive."

"Aggressive—what does that mean?" A muscle jerks in Seth's sharp-edged jaw as if he's heard the words but refuses them.

"It means it's already too late," Lacey whispers.

Sal shushes her. "Stop."

Lacey squeezes her eyes shut. "It means you die."

"Stop it," Sal says.

"I understand this is scary, Lacey." Mayr keeps his eyes on

hers. "But your type of cancer has a ninety-eight percent survival rate. And it's only in the one breast."

"What's the treatment plan?" Sal asks, pushing the conversation forward.

"We'd recommend a lumpectomy, which is a surgery that removes the cancer and other abnormal tissue from your breast. A lumpectomy allows you to keep the shape of your breast. It's not as invasive as a mastectomy."

Oh God.

Lacey's brain fizzes, overheats as Mayr goes on to detail the procedure. The cold, clinical medical terms being hurled at her sound like gibberish. How can anyone do this? How did her mother do this?

"After the surgery," Mayr says, and Lacey blinks herself back, "we'd do radiation. Possibly, we might recommend tamoxifen. It's an oral medication that lowers the risk of recurrence." Mayr pauses. "That is if you don't plan on having children for several years."

"I don't—" Lacey's shoulders sag as her mind wheels. Asking her to make decisions about her future, her body, when she doesn't even know. "I—" Eyes wide, she looks at Seth.

His handsome face is stone.

Keeping his eyes trained on Mayr, Seth says, "Whatever it takes, Doctor. The best surgeons. Medicine. You give her anything she needs." He looks at Lacey, clasping her hands. "I don't care about kids. I don't need 'em."

Her eyes shutter at his heartbreaking words. She shakes her head slowly. "Seth . . ."

"Princess, you get what you need." He cups her face, turns toward her like there aren't two more people in the room. Like her world isn't ending. "*You* are what I need, you hear me? Nothin' else. You."

Before she can say anything, Seth looks at Mayr, his expression fierce. "After the surgery, she'll be okay, right?"

"I assure you she'll have the very best team at the hospital to take care of her." Mayr hesitates. "There is always the chance we get in there and find more that wasn't present on the imaging. It could change her treatment."

Lacey hears the unsaid. *And her chances.*

Apparently so does Seth.

"Wait. What?" Seth asks, his handsome face rigid with pain.

Lacey's eyes sting with unshed tears. If she never sees a worse sight, it'll be Seth's face in this moment, crumpling.

It's like a bad joke at the wrong, the very worst time. She and Seth were planning a wedding, and now . . .

Now what?

"I think," Sal says, speaking up before Seth can completely lose it, "we should take this one step at a time and get Lacey on the schedule. Soon." She leans forward to look at Lacey. Her smile is teary. "This is good news."

As Dr. Mayr launches into specifics and details, Lacey sits there, numb.

Hope.

She doesn't feel that.

Any of it.

Thirty minutes later, Seth and Lacey leave the hospital with pamphlets and order forms for Lacey's surgery in three weeks' time. As he guides her to the Bronco, her heels click-clacking on the cool asphalt, Seth flashes back to Los Angeles, taking Lacey home after her mugging.

His gut twists. He shouldn't be back here, doing this. He should be at home with Lacey in bed, making her feel good, not here watching the woman he loves fall apart. Because ever since they left Dr. Mayr's office, she hasn't said a word.

He knows she's scared.

Hell, he's fucking terrified.

There's poison in her body. Something foreign and monstrous

threatening to grow, to take her from him. He wants to find it and rip it the fuck out of her. Make it his. But he can't do any of that.

Utterly fucking helpless is what he is.

They climb into the Bronco. Lacey curls up against the passenger-side door, her green eyes far away as Seth rips the Bronco out of the parking spot.

Lacey clutches at her necklace. Taps the window as Seth catches a dark shadow scramble across the sidewalk. "Someone from the *Star*."

Seth swears, tempted to back up and drive over the guy. Motherfuckers publish photos of Lacey, he's gonna sue the shit out of that tabloid right before he burns it to the ground.

Lacey sighs, tired. For minutes, they drive in silence, passing over the overpass and then the byway back to their apartment.

Seth's eyes flick to Lacey. "How do you feel?"

Her cracked voice breaks the silence. "Guess we're working on the sickness part first."

A muscle clenches in Seth's jaw. "Don't do that."

She sighs. "I'm sorry. I'm just . . ." Tears fill her eyes. "I'm sad, Seth."

"I know. And you can be sad." He finds her hand, his heart swelling as her slender fingers curl into his. "I'm sad as hell, Lace. But what you got from the doctor, it's good news, princess. The best."

She bites her lip. "Are you worried?"

He wants to lie, but he doesn't. "Yeah. I am."

He's grateful they got lucky and caught it early. He is.

But he's also scared as shit.

That this wrecks Lacey. That surgery doesn't go as planned. That it comes back.

Still, he's gotta have hope. He's gotta hang on.

The news could be worse. It could be dark. And it would end him.

But Lacey's got more than a good chance, and he's determined to be her light. Because he knows, even though the news is good, it came out of left field to upend her—and his—entire world. She'll get better, but not without a lot of attention and medicine and pain. The next three years will be getting her the treatment she needs.

Just like that their life changed.

"I don't even know how to do this," Lacey whispers. She takes a deep, shuddering breath, then bursts out: "I don't *want* to do it. And then I feel selfish because I have to. Because it's not *that* bad, but to me, it's awful. It's scary, Seth."

"It is." His throat bobs painfully.

She's sick.

His girl is sick.

And he can't protect her.

The thought has the power to put him in the grave.

"I have to have surgery," she hisses. "My breast will never be the same. And if it comes back . . ." Her eyes squeeze shut against the thought.

Seth's knuckles are white on the wheel. He shakes his head, because the thought of anything happening to Lacey has him slowly combusting. "It won't come back."

"We don't know that," she says in a dull voice.

He glances over. He can see the desperation and doubt coming off her in waves. His hurricane girl is barely a breeze. Christ. He'd kill to get that fierce fire, that fight back in her green eyes.

All he can do is show her that he's still in this, that he loves her. That he isn't going anywhere.

Show her that he isn't going to stop planning their future and he hopes like hell she knows that.

An idea hitting him, Seth slows on the gas.

"Hang on, princess."

With a jerk of the wheel, Seth cranks the Bronco and flips a U-turn in the middle of the byway. Lacey squeals, gripping the Oh Shit handle above the door for dear life.

When they've cleared the intersection, she straightens up, half-laughing, half-scowling. The smile on her face has his chest unclenching its stranglehold. "Seth, are you crazy?" Her eyes scan the road signs. "Where are we going?"

"We ain't goin' home." Seth merges left, speeding up to take the road to Luke's. "I wanna show you somethin.'"

Lacey sits up in the passenger seat when Wild Antler Farm comes into view. When she looks at Seth quizzically, he says, "Sit tight, princess."

Intrigued, she does.

Instead of taking the main road to Sal and Luke's house, the Bronco continues straight for about two miles, then hooks a left on a snaky trail of back road. Lacey bounces in her seat, laughing as Seth cranks the radio to an old country song and sings along in a hokey warble, his deep voice a soothing rumble of happy.

Relief washes over her. Instantly, she feels better. Because that's Seth. Always making sure they can get through anything, get through it together.

She needs this man. So damn much.

Minutes later, the Bronco comes to a stop on top of a hill. Seth hops out, hustles to her side and opens her door. After helping her out, he leads her to a spot where the grass is overrun. Tall oak trees line the ridge; a deer darts past a shrub. Off in the distance, she can see Wild Antler Farm, the sparkling river.

Standing there, Lacey takes it all in. The beauty of the country, the wild fragrant scent of grass and sun. She feels like she's a world away from reality, nestled in the forest.

"It's so peaceful out here," she says, her hand tangled with Seth's.

He squeezes her tight. "You like it?"

"I do." She inclines her head, sweeping a lock of hair from her face. "Seth, where are we?"

"We're on our land. If you want it."

Her eyes widen in surprise. She looks across the countryside. Looks back at Seth. "I don't understand."

"I've been meanin' to talk to you about it . . . but with everything that's happened I damn near forgot." His smile crinkles the corner of his eyes. "A weddin' present from Luke and Sal."

Lacey gasps as he gestures out at the land.

"It's their property. But it could be ours. I know we've been lookin' for houses, but we could build something. Right here." Turning into her, his hands cup her face, his calloused thumbs sweeping over her cheekbones. "I wanna build something for you, Lace. Something perfect. A house you deserve."

Stunned, she stares up at him. While her brain screams at her to be reasonable—the future's unknown, foolish girl—her heart wants to hope. Wants to live. Wants to fight.

A lump forms in her throat and she turns her eyes toward the overgrown land. She never pictured herself living in the country, has always been a city girl, but there's something so right about this land. For so long, Wild Antler Farm was her sanctuary . . . and now this spot . . .

It pulls at her.

A feeling of peace, of contentment, breaks through her worry and woe.

Her and Seth—they could live here. A mere mile from her sister and their family. Make their home the weekend spot for bonfires, for front porch talks, for picking parties, and suddenly, Lacey can picture their life here.

At her silence, Seth shifts, his face adorably nervous. "It don't have to be here, though. Wherever you want, princess. Mansion or doublewide, I'll get it."

Lacey immediately starts to shake her head. "No." She grabs his shirt. "Here. I love it here."

His ocean-blue eyes shine. "Good."

"I feel safe here," she admits, tilting her head to take in the million-dollar view. "Like I could come to this spot when everything's wrong and somehow it would all be okay."

"It *will* be okay." Pain rolls over Seth's handsome face, but as quick as it comes, it's gone, confidence and determination settling in. "This is a lot, I know it is, but, princess, we'll get through it." His voice breaks. "I love you so goddamn much. I'm here, by your side, and I ain't leavin'. I'm with you, Lace. This is our fight together."

Tears fill her eyes at the strength, the certainty in his voice. "I know you are."

Seth steps closer to tuck her into his strong arms. His mouth lowers to the crown of her head, his sweet kiss sweeping over her. "We take it one day at a time. One breath, one heartbeat at a time, okay, princess?"

She tips back to look up at him, hope burning a fire through her. "We do. We will."

She inhales the cool March air, letting his comforting words reassure her.

She is okay. She is here with Seth.

Curling into his arms, she asks, "Now what?"

He grins. "We got a piece of dirt, princess. Now we build."

He pulls her into him, not letting her loose. Lacey rests her head on his shoulder as they stare out on their land, syncing breaths, heartbeats, lives.

With Seth she feels steady. Healthy.

In Seth's arms, right here, right now, it feels like everything will be okay.

# chapter SEVEN

"LACEY SUTTON?"

Lacey nods as the woman at the bridal store gives her a big bright smile. "That's me. I got a call saying my dresses are in."

"Right. I'll pull them." The woman's eyes widen as she reads Lacey's file. "Oh! The *Kincaid* wedding." She lifts a hand, signaling someone, and gives Lacey a knowing smile. "Please have a seat, Ms. Sutton. We'll bring out some champagne. My name is Mel, and please let me know if you need anything at all."

Lacey sits on a plush pink couch. Decadence surrounds her. A white dreamland filled with gauze and iridescent veils and sparkly tiaras and hopes and love and dreams. Lacey wishes she had brought Sal, but her sister's doing so much for her, she doesn't want to burden her with anything else.

While she waits, her wedding magazines and planner stacked beside her, Lacey thumbs through her work emails and fires off a text to a potential new client. Normally, she's off Sundays, but she spent all day notifying her clients about her upcoming surgery and time off and putting the finishing touches on Alabama's party. And then it's off to Sal and Luke's for Sunday supper.

She keeps thinking about how strange it is to be living her normal life, when it's been anything but. The first days after her diagnosis felt like a fog. But she forced herself through it, and now, she's running on automatic pilot with her breath held.

Wake. Walk. Work. Repeat. All she can do to focus, to feel normal.

Because she needs to be normal. She needs not to think about how she doesn't have control. All she has is unknowns and it terrifies her.

The only thing helping her get through it is Seth. His steadying words.

*We take it one day at a time. One breath, one heartbeat at a time, okay, princess?*

Okay.

"And here we are." The chirp of a voice has Lacey glancing up.

Mel's returned, wheeling in a delicate clothing rack. Three dresses hang in bright pink sparkly garment bags. Pre-ceremony. Ceremony. After-party. A shiver of anticipation goes through Lacey at seeing her dresses. While she worked on her dresses with a local designer, nothing will compare to seeing the finished product in lieu of sketches.

God, she can't wait for Seth to see her in them.

"They came in at the perfect time," Mel says, unzipping the first bag with careful ease. "You're about three months out, right?"

"I am. Oh." Breath catching in her throat, Lacey sets down her champagne and stands.

Mel, seeing her dumbfounded expression, smiles. "Beautiful, isn't it?"

"It is," Lacey says, staring at her pre-ceremony dress. A blush-colored satin spaghetti-strap slip dress. Slowly, she walks around it, taking it in from every gorgeous angle. With a plunging neckline and thigh-high slit, the gown's sexy and sultry and—

"Remind me again. Were you planning to go braless?"

Blinking, Lacey looks up. "Excuse me?"

Smiling kindly, Mel gestures at Lacey. "Well, you're petite and could go without for this dress. But if retaining some of your breasts' look and shape is important to you, we can bring in our own vendors for a custom fit."

Oh God.

Lacey's heart drops into her high heels, any joy she felt at seeing her dresses immediately sideswiped.

She never even thought about her breasts and her bras and her wedding dress. Dr. Mayr had mentioned maybe a small scar or an uneven pit, everything fixable with plastic surgery, but even that wasn't for sure.

*Nothing's for sure,* Lacey thinks.

Not her breasts. Not her future.

Nothing.

In that second, Lacey's hit with a horrible realization. Every aspect of her life will be touched by cancer. Her loved ones. Her future. Her health. It'll sneak out of the cracks when she least expects it, but it'll be there. Ready to wreak havoc on her heart, her happiness.

"We can try these on now, but for future fittings, you'll need your bras." Mel gives her a conspiratorial look and turns to unzip the second garment bag. "Now this one is my favorite—"

"I have to go," Lacey blurts, backing away from the dresses.

"Is something wrong?"

"I'm fine. I just—" Lacey tucks a lock of hair behind her ears, dipping down to grab up her belongings. She blanches, finding a cancer pamphlet stuck between the pages of *The Knot* magazine, amplifying her already spastic thoughts. She nearly rockets to standing, slinging her bag over her shoulder. "I just remembered I have an appointment. I can't do this right now."

She doesn't spare Mel, or her dresses, a final glance as she rushes out of the bridal store. The bag on her shoulder, holding her magazines and ready-to-be-mailed wedding invitations, feels about a hundred pounds.

Tears begin to run down Lacey's cheeks.

Heavy. Everything's too heavy.

"You tryin' to stare a hole in the window?" Sal asks from behind Seth, passing him a babbling Cash.

Seth grunts softly and juggles the baby in his arms. "Waitin' on Lace."

He's well aware he's acting like an overbearing asshole, but he's worried about her. He wants her safe and happy and healthy and he'll damn well do anything he needs to do to make sure she gets there.

His vow to her.

One day at a time. One breath. One heartbeat.

He hands Cash the salt shaker, which Cash immediately dumps on the front of Seth's shirt.

Seth stares, impressed. "For some reason I didn't think you'd actually do it." He tickles Cash's chubby toes. "That's kinda on me, kid."

Laughing, Sal checks the clock on the wall. "She's later than normal."

"Her dresses came in today," Seth says with a chuckle. "She's probably camped out at the boutique."

Sal's eyes widen. "They did? She didn't tell me that."

"She probably forgot," Seth says, in an effort to make her feel better.

Sal hesitates, reaching across the ready-to-eat salad to move the peach pie away from Cash's handsy grab. "How's she doing?"

"She's workin'," Seth grumbles. Cash lets out a screech as if to emphasize his point. "Too damn much."

He knows it's Lacey's way, bury herself in work, but he ain't happy about it. He wants her to slow down, to take doctor's advice and rest and get enough sleep, but she'll be damned if she stops.

Sal gives him a look of sympathy. Pats his hand. "The doctors caught it early, Seth. She'll be okay." A shaky shudder rockets out of her as if she's trying to convince herself. "I know it."

Heat building behind his eyes, Seth stares at his best friend and squeezes her hand. "You saved her life, Sal."

The honest truth. An awful thought. A thought he's had about a million times since Lacey got her diagnosis. He thanks Christ Sal dragged her to that appointment. If she hadn't . . .

A rough exhale rattles out of him. "Jesus. I can't even think about what would have happened if she waited—"

Sal tries to smile. "So don't. We'll get you through this. Everyone's here."

He knows they are. In the last week, Emmy Lou and Alabama have sent flowers, dropped off food. Griff left a bottle of whiskey at their front door. Sal and Luke have invited them over for dinner every night, steering clear of any hard talk about Lacey's diagnosis unless she broaches the subject. Everyone in his country music family trying to help, trying to take their minds off it in their own way.

Nodding, throat tight, Seth leans in and smacks a kiss against Cash's cherubic cheek. "Can't cry if a baby's here. It's the law, ain't it, kid?"

Sal arches a brow at her son. "Think Cash has got crying down for all of us."

Seth looks up, meeting Sal's misty green eyes. He needs to say this. Wants his best friend to know how much his heart is in this. "I'm going to take care of her, Sal."

Sal holds his gaze, then she smiles. "I know you will."

The back screen door slams and Luke strides in, beer in hand. Winston, Sal's scrappy terrier, skitters beside him, begging for a handout. "Burgers are done," he announces, tongs raised in victory.

"We're waiting on Lacey," Sal says, uncorking a bottle of wine. From the living room, the record player croons Merle Haggard. An early-evening spring breeze flutters the curtains.

Seth straightens up, Cash cradled in his arms. "Kid and I were just talkin' about how the Brothers Kincaid wouldn't even be a band if it weren't for me."

Sal laughs and Luke snakes his arms around her waist, pulling her back against his chest. "Don't listen to your uncle," he says to Cash. "I can play a little violin."

Seth cackles, his rumble of a laugh surprising even him. "Kid, your dad's a liar." He raises an eyebrow at Sal. "He ever tell you how he popped every string on my fiddle?"

Sal gasps, twisting in Luke's arms to look up at him. "No. But now it's a story I need to hear."

"Asshole," Luke says, giving Seth a glare.

Seth opens his mouth, but before he can launch into specifics, there's the clatter of the screen door. Lacey struts in on her high heels.

He grins. "Saved by the princess."

Lacey smiles, but it doesn't reach her eyes. She looks weary and frazzled, standing with her arms folded tightly beneath her breasts.

"How'd the fitting go?" Sal asks, sliding Lacey a glass of wine.

Lacey shrugs. "Fine." She walks to Seth, gives him a kiss, and then steals Cash from his arms. "I didn't have time to try the dresses on," she says, burrowing her face in Cash's shoulder and inhaling his scent. "I saw them and they look beautiful, but I just . . . I'll go back."

Sal gapes at her dispirited sister. Seth finds himself doing the same thing.

Lacey passing up a dress fitting ain't happening.

Seth watches Lacey's hand grip the stem of the wineglass Sal's passed her. It's shaking.

He puts his hands on her shoulders. "You okay?"

"I'm fine, Seth," she says softly, but she's staring down at Cash. A long beat of silence. Then, like she's kicking herself into another gear, she snaps to attention, her shoulders soldier-straight. "Should we eat? Here." She passes Cash to Luke. "I'll help set the table."

Then, with a toss of her long blond hair, Lacey grabs up the salad, turns on the ball of her high-heeled shoe and struts out of the room. A woof rumbling out of him, Winston skitters after her.

Seth meets Sal's worried eyes, but slowly they all follow Lacey into the living room.

Luke puts on another record. More wine is poured. Luke, Sal, Seth and Lacey sit at the long table, dinner finished, the night noise swelling around them. By Sal's elbow sits the baby monitor, where, on-screen, Cash sleeps easy in his crib upstairs.

A little wine, a little whiskey, and Lacey's relaxed. The incident from earlier today out of her mind.

Well, almost.

She needed this. This great night with her family, relaxing. Forgetting. Not so serious for once.

Luke sits back in his chair, stretching his arm across Sal's shoulders, and says to Lacey, "Seth says you saw the land."

"I did. I love it."

Sal smiles, claps her hands together in delight. "We're going to be neighbors."

Lacey laughs. "Get ready to be sick of me."

"Too late," Luke teases, and she sticks her tongue out at him.

Lacey hugs her hands to her chest. "I can already picture the bathroom now."

Seth cackles, then straightens up and takes a sip of his whiskey. "Already got bids from some architects too."

The table falls quiet. Luke and Lacey blink. "Already?" Lacey asks. It's news to her.

"Sure did, princess." He gives her a cocky grin that curls her toes. "We can get to drawin' up the plans any day now."

"A weddin', a house?" Luke whistles. "That's a lot, Seth." He looks worried, but Sal squeezes his arm.

"Gotta get the show on the road," Seth swaggers, only Lacey sits silent, her heart pumping double time.

She loves Seth, loves him for thinking of the future, for moving their life along when she's barely hanging on. But suddenly the list of things to do seems so endless. So futile.

All at once she's flashing back to today. Replaying every ounce of uncertainty over something so small, something so trivial like a bra. But it isn't trivial. It's her life.

Lacey breathes in, breathes out, focusing on the chatter of conversation to calm herself.

Seth leans in, a hand on her shoulder, and Lacey does her best not to jump out of her skin.

"You feel okay?" he murmurs in a low tone.

She turns to him. "Seth, if you keep asking me that I will drown you in the Cumberland."

Normally, she'd find his fussing adorable. Yet after the day she's had, it's suffocating. She wants to be normal, not coddled.

"I'm fine," she explains with a sniff. "It was a long day."

Seth shakes his head. "Shouldn't be workin' on a Sunday anyway."

Lacey sighs and taps a manicured nail against her wineglass. "I have to work, Seth. I have clients I need to finish up with before my surgery. At the very least let them all know I'd be out."

"They understand, at least?" Luke asks, refilling Sal's wine.

"They do. I told them I'd be back to work a week after my surgery."

"Lacey . . ." Sal exhales and looks to Seth.

Seth groans and smears a hand down his face. "Princess, you are gonna kill me." He raises his gaze to hers and she sees the worry in his eyes. "You ain't weak for takin' time off, Lace."

Her nostrils flare. This isn't what she wants to be doing right now. Talking about being sick.

"Oh no," Sal whispers, interrupting their stare down. The baby monitor crackles. Both she and Luke watch it with intense concentration. Finally, Luke breathes easy as Cash's whimpers fade to silence.

Seth chuckles, says, "Kid's got you runnin' scared."

"He's finally sleeping through the night." Sal keeps her panicked eyes on the monitor. "We can't jinx this."

Luke's eyes are laughing but serious. "Keep talkin' and I'll send you up there," he says to Seth.

Lacey yawns, then laughs. "You do that, you'll never get him back down."

Seth, noticing Lacey's yawn, says, "Speakin' of sleep, we should get home."

Lacey scoffs and resets her expression. "Don't be silly. We can stay." She smiles at Sal. "I am having wine tonight and I am staying up."

A muscle jerks in Seth's jaw. He hasn't taken his eyes off her. "Oh, that's a good idea." His voice is tight, his handsome smile slipping. "What you need to be is exhausted."

"What I need," Lacey says, taking a large gulp of wine, "is to be here with my family."

"The doctor said—"

"I know what the doctor said, Seth. I was there, remember?"

His jaw hardens, his ocean-blue eyes burning with concern.

Luke tenses, his eyes moving to Sal, who sits frozen.

They don't fight.

Bicker, yes. Banter, always. But fight . . . not like this. Lacey knows Seth's only coming from a place of love and concern, but she doesn't want it like this.

She doesn't want any of this.

But before she can say so, apologize for snapping, explain her anxiety, Seth puts a broad hand out, his handsome expression twisted. "Can you just do this one thing for me so I can fuckin' sleep tonight?"

"God, Seth." Lacey laughs bitterly. "Relax. I'm not going to die if I stay out past ten o'clock."

It's the absolute worst thing she can say.

Her words suck the air from the room.

Sal pales and Luke goes deathly still, his eyes locking on his brother.

And Seth . . .

Seth sits rigid, the hard bob of his throat telling her she's hurt him.

Pain rolls over Seth's face and he looks at her as if he's about to get up and leave. But he doesn't. Because Lacey gets there first.

Her hand darts out and she catches his shirt sleeve. "Seth. I didn't—" Words failing her, wide-eyed, she looks around the table.

Then, Seth's soft drawl, a hand on her back. "I know." His voice so comforting, so forgiving, she wants to break into tears.

Luke's already standing, pulling Sal up with him. "Let's give 'em a sec, darlin'," he says, taking her hand and the baby monitor. Sal follows him out, her expression one of sympathy.

Tears in her eyes, Lacey hangs her head. "I'm so sorry, Seth. I never should have said that."

"You ain't gotta be," Seth says, turning in his chair to face her.

She wipes her eyes, sniffs. "I'm such a mess. And Sal and Luke—"

"Sal and Luke don't care. You know that." Seth stares at her, his eyes filling with confusion. "What's wrong, princess?"

"I had a bad day," she says, scooting her chair closer to him.

Seth wraps her up in his arms and she melts into him. He kisses the crown of her blond head. "You can have a bad day."

"I don't want bad days. And I don't want to take my bad days out on you." She lays her head against his shoulder, hating herself for hurting him. "I want things to go back to normal." A long silence, Seth rubbing her back, and then Lacey inhales a deep breath, says, "I needed a bra for my dress fitting."

Seth sighs, and she can hear the rush of air, a comforting rumble rolling through his body and into Lacey's.

"And all I could think about is what type of bra? How will my breast look after surgery? What if I look awful?" She closes her eyes. "I think I can do my day, and there there's always something that makes me remember what's coming. That nothing is normal. That I'm broken."

"You ain't broken, Lace."

"I just . . . don't want us to fall apart."

"Hell, that's the last thing we're doin'." A finger beneath her chin, tipping her gaze up to meet his. Her heart stops. There's so much pain, so much fierce determination, it steals her breath. "We ain't seen our best days, princess. I can promise you that."

"Yeah, but . . . all this . . ." She shakes her head. "The house. The wedding. The surgery. It's so much."

"It is, but I got it taken care of." Seth squeezes her tight. "And I'll take care of you."

His words send hope and love blazing through her chest.

Bad days. They can shake off bad days. They can do this.

Together.

*One breath, one heartbeat at a time . . .*

Then Seth kisses her, kisses her with a desperation to be closer to her, to show her how much she means to him. Asking her to believe him.

"Don't push me away," he whispers against her lips. "Please, princess."

Lacey whimpers and runs her hands through his hair, pulling him closer. "I won't," she says, and she means it.

Tries to.

# *chapter* EIGHT

IT'S BEEN A DAMN LONG DAY.

Seth sits in a Six String boardroom waiting to have a conference call with an overseas tour venue that Bobby arranged. So far there've been no signs of Luke, Jace or Bobby, which is just fine with him because his mind is anywhere but the music.

It's on Lacey.

In front of him, spread across the glossy dark table, are proposals from architects. Pamphlets from the cancer center. The cartoon illustrations, the robotic instructions piss him off. Like it's that easy.

Like the love of his life isn't in pain.

Like he doesn't hear her crying in the bathroom everything morning, lying awake beside him every night.

With a tired groan, Seth smears his face in his hands.

After the blowup at Sal and Luke's, both of them have been doing their damnedest to keep on keepin' on. At night, he and Lacey come together, Lacey whispering she loves him, needs him, but despite her promise, despite the love they make, he can feel her pulling away. *Pushing* him away. There's no wedding talk. She's working every hour she can, running on coffee and the highest heels he's ever seen. A coping mechanism he saw firsthand in LA. Working her ass off to stay sane.

And all he can do is watch her go.

He gets it. He's doing the same thing.

Burning both ends to keep the faith. Reading these pamphlets, building a house, it's what he can do to take charge. To not feel so goddamn helpless. So full of rage.

It's either this or go to that same dark place he went after he got Luke hurt.

He can't go there again. There ain't no damn way. Not with Lacey to take care of.

His job is to stay steady for her when everything inside of him feels shook up and stomped on. Do everything he can to push their life forward. To get her healthy. To show her their future won't stop or end, that he's right there beside her.

Because he knows what she's thinking. How do you go on with a normal life when it feels like the noose could drop at any time?

His eyes fall to the pamphlet about post-surgery care. Seth has read and researched and knows this shit inside and out. Hell, if Lacey has to go through it, he's gonna know everything too. He'll be damned if she goes through this alone.

It's bad enough she's at the doctor right now getting poked and prodded for her upcoming surgery. The testing's complicated, drawing blood, scanning for autoimmune diseases to get a picture of her overall health. He should be with her, but Lacey claimed Sal's better at the medical stuff. Another way she's pushing him away. She doesn't want him to worry.

She doesn't want him around.

The thought rips him apart from the inside out.

The loud crack of the door has Seth's head snapping up. Luke and Jace. They stop. Stare at the pamphlets and plans spread out across the table next to Seth's fiddle case.

Luke's eyes widen at Seth's appearance. "You look like shit."

"I remember this with Sal," Seth says with a grin. Trying to keep that same swagger everyone expects. "Except it's you chasin' me this time."

Luke frowns.

Jace settles beside him. "How's Lacey doin'?"

Seth shrugs. "She's Lacey. Runnin' scared. She won't talk to me. She won't eat and she sure as hell ain't sleepin.'"

"What about you?" Jace asks.

"What about me?"

"Seth." Luke's mouth is a flat white line. Both him and Jace are giving him that overly concerned raised eyebrow look.

Seth groans, fighting a yawn. "Surgery's in two weeks. I'll get her through it and then we'll both take a long-ass nap."

Jace frowns. "That's too damn long."

Seth grunts.

His friend is right.

Though he tries to keep the grim thoughts at bay, Seth's on edge. Worrying about Lacey's upcoming surgery. What if they've waited too long? What if they're too late? What if they open her up and—

Shaking off his dark thoughts, Seth looks up at Luke, who's leaning back against the boardroom table. "We doin' this call or what?" he asks, drumming his fingers on the table. Ready to get this boring business shit out of the way and make it back to Lacey. If he can meet her at the hospital, maybe he won't feel like such a worthless asshole for not being there today.

"Not today," Luke says. "I rescheduled it."

Seth stares. His brother blowing off music business is like hell freezing over. It just doesn't happen. "Hell, Luke, you feelin' okay?"

Luke snorts, then sits beside him. "You're doin' too much." His dark eyes scour over Seth. "You can't have a weddin', build a house, and—"

Luke's next words trail off, but Seth doesn't miss the look that passes between Jace and Luke. Doesn't miss the unsaid words.

*Take care of Lacey.*

With a shake of his head, Seth slaps shut a pamphlet. A muscle works in his jaw. Conviction blasts a hole in his heart.

"She's gonna be okay."

"She will be," Luke says softly. "No one's sayin' otherwise.

But you gotta be okay too." He clasps Seth's shoulder. Squeezes. "You eat today?"

Seth doesn't think he or Lacey has. Hell, Seth walked out of the house today in just his socks. Not like he'd tell Luke that.

Luke jerks his head to the door. "C'mon. Let's get a beer and a burger."

Minutes later, the Brothers Kincaid are striding down the sidewalk, bypassing glossy high-rises and the bustling Broadway crowd of tourists and musicians. Seth catches his haggard appearance reflected at him from a blacked-out window.

Fuck. So, this is why Luke is worried.

As they pass Tootsie's, a woman pushes off the purple brick wall and follows. "Excuse me, Seth Kincaid?"

Seth glances back at the call of his name. A sound of disgust from Luke.

"Just keep walkin'," Jace mutters, grabbing his shoulder and propelling him forward.

"Seth, I was wondering if you could answer some questions about your fiancée's condition. She's been seen at the hospital and we're wondering if we could have a comment."

Seth stops next to a red brick building, Luke nearly running over him. Fists clenched, he turns around and narrows his gaze. The woman's petite, with long black hair and big blue eyes. Sweet-looking. But he knows better.

"Are you from the *Star*?"

She blinks. "Well, yes, I'm—"

"I don't care what your fuckin' name is." Seth jabs a finger. "Stay away from my wife."

She perks up. "Are you married?"

"We ain't, but I'm callin' her that because I'm marrying her in three damn months since you're so goddamn interested."

Luke steps to the right, getting in between them. His brother's face is strained. "Let's go, Seth."

The woman smiles. "Is she pregnant?"

A knife in his gut. "No fuckin' comment."

Turning away from the reporter, from Luke, Seth strides forward fast, wishing the reporter was a man, because if she was, she'd be on the ground right now.

His overprotective instincts are in overdrive. The last thing he wants for Lacey is this in the paper. She ought to be able to have her privacy, and it makes him goddamn sick he can't give that to her.

The voice follows him. A sharp shuffle of high heels.

"Is she sick?"

Seth stops. Turns.

"What'd you say?" His voice tumbles out like thunder.

A bark of warning from Luke. "Seth."

"Is she dying?"

The world slows. Rage bubbles in his veins.

Seething, fists clenched, he shakes his head and advances. "Lady, I am gonna ruin your fuckin' life."

With a harried glance at Luke, Jace steps into Seth's path, blocking him from going any further.

"Seth," Luke snaps, grabbing Seth's jacket in his fist. "Knock it off."

Seth twists in his brother's tight grip, still looking at the woman. "Stop followin' me and stop takin' pictures of Lacey. She ain't sick. She's fine. Leave her alone." His voice is a shout and people stop to stare. "Do you hear me? Do you fuckin' hear me?"

"Seth." Luke pushes him back, pain in his expression as he gives him a shake. "This ain't helpin'. Shut the fuck up."

The woman smirks and nods her head. "Thanks for the comment, Mr. Kincaid."

"Go!" Luke yells at the woman, anger burning bright in his dark eyes. "Get the hell out of here!"

The woman pauses as if she's about to say something else, but then she turns and walks back down the block.

Out of Jace, a hiss. "Bitch."

Luke immediately lets Seth loose and steps back.

"Fuck," Seth swears, his gut knotting. He rips a hand through his hair and turns away, breathing heavily.

It feels like there's a rope around his throat.

Squeezing the life out of him, the hope.

Jace and Luke's low voices sound like they're underwater.

*Is she dying?*

*Is she?*

And that's when Seth gets it.

Lacey ain't made of steel or heaven. She's a body. A breath. The woman he writes into every one of his songs. The woman he loves more than life itself. The woman he could lose.

*No.*

*Christ, no.*

The demolition of his heart doesn't even take ten seconds.

Seth squeezes his eyes shut.

The world blurs. Blackness. Rage.

*Lacey.*

"Fuck!" Seth shouts.

And then he opens his eyes, balls his hand, and slams a fist into the brick wall.

Lacey makes tea.

That is, she would if her sister stopped her hovering.

"Don't." Lacey points at Sal as she moves to rise with the siren of the tea kettle. She's so damn sick of everyone treating her like she's breakable. "I can lift a teapot, Sal."

Shamefaced, Sal sinks back into her seat. "I know. Sorry." Then she smiles, the serious edge chased away from her pretty face. "Payback."

Lacey allows herself a chuckle, flips off the burner. God, was she this bad when Sal came home?

Glancing over her shoulder, she eyes Sal. "I know I—"

"Hovered. Smothered."

Lacey gasps in indignation. "Yes. But I did all of that because—"

"You love me, and I love you, and this is what we do, get it?"

Lacey sighs, glances down at the gauze wrapped around her elbow, courtesy of her recent blood draw. "I get it."

Earlier today, she and Sal spent all afternoon at the hospital, where she completed all her labs and signed her consent for surgery. She gave so many vials of blood, her right arm could double as a pincushion.

Minutes later, Lacey sets a pot of tea down on the table, then sits across from Sal. Lacey fixes her big sister with a look. "You have a baby, Sal. You should be at home with him, not babysitting me until Seth gets home."

"Cash will be fine with the nanny for a few more hours." Sal pours Lacey a cup of tea. "Let people help you, Lace. Everyone came together for me. We want to for you."

Lacey bites her lip at the concern in her sister's words. And she finds herself wishing her sister would leave, not because she doesn't love her, but because she can't take Sal fussing. She's learning how to fully open up, and all this does is make her want to shut down.

Most days, she's struggling between laughing and weeping at the ridiculousness of it all. Living her life while slowly freaking out. She feels hollow and exhausted, like she's standing in front of a door she needs to open, but she keeps missing the knob, over and over.

Still, Lacey's determined to be positive if it kills her. She knows a good mindset is a necessity. She has a good man, good friends and family, but . . . what if . . . ?

It's the what-ifs that get her.

Lacey looks into her tea. Then says, "I'm mad, Sal."

"I know you are."

Looking up, Lacey juts her chin and says, "And I'm scared."

"I'm scared too. Seth's scared. Your friends are scared." Sal takes her hand. "But we are going to kick cancer's ass. And in a year or two, it'll all be behind you."

She stares at Sal, weighing whether to say it, and then she lets it out in one long breath of a ramble. "Sometimes I feel like if I let my guard down and believe everything will be okay, it won't be. And I'm terrified of that, Sal. I want to be positive for Seth, for myself, but . . . what if it's not?"

Her words make Sal pause for a moment. "You're right," her sister says finally. "I get it, Lacey. I do."

"What would Mom say?"

Sal chuckles. "You're asking me?"

"I am." She needs words from her mother, even if they're not directly from her.

Sal thinks on it. "She'd say . . . if you fall off the board, you get back on, and then you paddle your ass back into that ocean and try again." With a laugh, Sal buries her face in her hand, peeks out at Lacey through her fingers with an almost embarrassed smile. "I don't know. Does that sound right?"

"Yeah," Lacey breathes. Heat builds behind her eyes. "That sounds perfect."

Dropping her hand, Sal clears her throat, the sheen of tears in her eyes fading. "How are you and Seth doing?"

"We're okay. Working a lot." Lacey smiles, but it feels tight on her face. "He's interviewing a few architects," she says, gesturing at the business cards Seth's collected.

Where happiness should be, there's only guilt. Seth's done nothing but reassure her. Nothing but work his ass off and miss practice and put her first.

"And the wedding?"

Lacey's smile falters. Another topic she'd like to change. "It's . . . going."

"I haven't gotten an invitation."

"I haven't mailed them."

Sal stares at her. "According to the schedule you handed out at your engagement party, they were due last week."

Lacey shifts in her seat, a warmth spreading up her neck. Warmth behind her eyes. "So they're late."

"You're never late. At least not with a party." Sal shakes her head. "What about the shower? I thought we could—"

"I don't want a shower, Sal." She says it too fast, too sharp.

Sal sits frozen. Wide-eyed. Stunned. "You don't want to marry Seth?" Her voice is cloudy like she might start crying then and there.

"I do." Lacey glances down at her now-cold tea. Whispers, "I just, I don't think I should. I think we should postpone the wedding."

A thought that's been rattling around in her brain more often than she wants to admit.

She's unsure. Never about Seth, but about what *he's* getting into. What kind of life is Seth in for? Sure, her diagnosis isn't doomed, but what if the cancer comes back? What if there's no hope next time? What if he turns into her father?

What if he leaves her?

Everything in her life feels push-pull.

She wants the surgery, but she's so afraid of what they'll find.

She wants to marry Seth, but planning the wedding feels fruitless. Exhausting.

She wants to have hope, but she's so damn scared to believe in the future.

"Does he know this?" Sal asks.

She swallows. "No."

Her sister blows out a sharp breath. "Lacey. Talk to me."

Tears sting Lacey's eyes, her heart a tumbleweed in her chest, and then she bursts out, "It's not fair to him. What if in the future it comes back? What if I have to do chemo like Mom and I'll lose my hair and Seth will leave me?"

"Lacey—"

"I plan parties, but I can't plan my way out of this." Tears drip into her tea. "No one can."

Sal looks her over carefully. "You have to talk to Seth, Lacey."

"I know. But I'm afraid. He's doing so much; I don't want to worry him with anything else. Or . . ." Her hands twist together, because the truth hurts. "What if he feels the same way?"

A sadness enters Sal's eyes and she shakes her head. "He won't. He loves you."

"Ugh," Lacey growls, swiping at tears. "I'm such a gross hot mess."

Sal chuckles. "It's okay to be. This is scary. And you can vent and rage and be unsure. But don't push Seth away. You need him. And he's—"

But she never gets to finish her sentence.

The front door slams open.

Lacey turns, her eyes widening at the scene. Seth's hand balled against his side, his handsome face twisted up in pain, Luke and Jace hauling him into the apartment.

"Oh my God. What happened?" Lacey asks, scrambling up.

"He punched a goddamn wall," Luke snaps, eyes wild, as he drags his brother to a chair. "Sit your ass down," he tells Seth.

"I'm fine," Seth says, looking up at Lacey. "I'm fine, princess."

"You're not fine," Lacey says, horrified. She leans over him to examine the damage, and he snakes an arm around her waist, tugging her toward him. Shocked, she rears back. "Seth, your hand—why would you—"

"Some lady at the *Star* was botherin' him. Askin' questions about Lacey," Jace explains in a low voice to Sal. "She said—"

"Jace," Seth growls, sending his bandmate a sharp glare, and Lacey stares. He looks weary and worried and so unlike the man she knows. "Shut the fuck up."

Turning his attention back to Lacey, Seth's eyes widen as he stares at the gauze wrapped around her elbow. "Christ. Your arm, Lace—"

"I don't care about my arm." Her heart thundering, she palms his scruffy jaw, forcing him to look at her. "Why'd you do this? Why, Seth?"

"Because he's an idiot," Luke thunders, but he sounds worried.

Lacey watches as Luke's eyes snap to Sal, a secret language passing between them, and it's all she needs to know.

Seth's worked up over her. Her cancer. Someone from the *Star* found out.

Seth grabs her, and she can feel the warmth of his hand as he palms the small of her back. His rough rumble shakes out. "It ain't nothin' for you to worry about, princess. I'll be okay."

But she is worried.

So worried.

Sal, scowling, goes to Seth. "Open your hand," she says, gentle, but no-nonsense. Hissing a breath, Seth does. Barely. His battered hand flexing and unflexing in an almost spastic motion.

The small space of the apartment's chaotic as Luke hands over an ice pack. Lacey backs away from the scene. She can feel her heartbeat, spasming in her chest, like she can't process what's happening right now.

Leaning down, Sal touches Seth's knuckles, carefully inspecting. Seth waves off their concern, his head bowed, a muscle in his jaw flexing.

Lacey stands, hands clutched to her heart, watching the man she loves fall apart, and yet no force in the world can stop it.

Except her.

She's doing this to him.

And she has to stop it.

# chapter NINE

LACEY STARES AT HER NAKED BODY IN THE MIRROR.

Her breasts feel like bombs. Like betrayal.

She's asked a lot from her body over the years. Put it through so much awful shit.

Now she's asking it to come through for her. To heal. To live.

She lifts her arm, probing at the tan skin. Since her diagnosis, her mind won't stop running. Does her arm hurt? Does her breast? Is she sicker than they think? What will they really find when they open her up?

God. She's a disaster.

On the daily, her mind cartwheels with ridiculous scenarios. She knows they are. And she absolutely can't tell Seth or Sal. They'll worry even more. And worry is one thing she wants to run fast away from.

She has to be strong.

She's got this.

She does.

The door opens. Seth steps inside. Resting his bandaged hand on the door frame, he stares at her naked body in mirror. Her hand on her breast. The jut of her ribs. The dark smudges under her eyes.

His throat works. "Lace . . ."

His blue eyes—usually laughing or mischievous—are soft. Sad.

Turning away from him, she drops her eyes and slips on her robe. The sight of Seth's eyes on her breasts, her body, feels like a judgment. She knows she's lost weight. She knows she's been close to a bad habit she used to have. That slip of control.

"We have to go to Alabama's party."

He sighs and steps up behind her. "Let's skip it." Wrapping his arms around her midsection, Seth buries his face into the back of her neck and inhales. "Stay in bed."

"I can't skip it, Seth. I planned it." She wiggles impatiently in his arms. "I want to go out. We need some fun."

For the first time in a long time, she feels a kernel of excitement. Of normality. Getting out, getting dressed up, feeling normal is what she needs to boost her spirits.

Seth's deep drawl fills the room. "You oughta eat something before we go."

She sighs.

He's hovering. He's scared. Her eyes moved to his bandaged hand. Nearly healed, but she still hasn't forgotten that awful scene from a few days ago.

*Her fault. All her fault.*

She aches to tell him. Her doubts about their wedding. Her fears about the future. Curl up in his arms and weep a river. But she doesn't want him to worry. The bandage on his hand tells her he's done enough already.

Lacey juts her chin. "There's food at the party."

"Then get dressed. Because we gotta be ready in five." Her mouth flies open only for Seth to spin her around and silence her protest with a kiss. "Move that gorgeous ass of yours."

Happiness rushes through Lacey. The mood lightened as only Seth can do. He tries so hard to make her feel good, feel better.

God, she loves him.

Seth grins at her. "Five minutes, princess. Then I'm leavin' without you."

Lacey gasps and grips his shirt collar. "That's a class action lawsuit."

He laughs the laugh she loves. Bright and booming and causing her heart to flip over in her chest.

"Tonight," she says, shaking off her worries and jamming a manicured nail in his chest, "we have fun."

With a whoop, Seth catches her up in his arms, kisses her again.

This. She can do this.

A night of normalcy. That's all she wants.

Lacey smiles as she surveys the brightly lit townhouse. After an hour of directing the florist and bartender, Alabama and Griff's small housewarming party is in full swing. Warm and alive and electric with friends and family. Music pumps from the speakers. A bartender slings custom-created cocktails and plain old whiskey for Griff. A small stage in a corner of the room, instruments laid out, waits for a picking party.

Though she's in her element, her nerves are also lit. It's the first time seeing all her friends in one place since her diagnosis. No one has said anything directly, but she can tell they all know. The way Griff gave her a good strong hug earlier, his gruff voice softer than normal whenever he calls her California. She can feel Seth's gaze on her. Watching, waiting, making sure she isn't working too hard.

She hates it. Hates everything about it.

"Presents by the bar," Lacey says to a guest, nodding toward a small stack of housewarming gifts.

"Oh Lord, Lacey," Alabama drawls, sneaking up behind her. "Stop workin.'"

"You're off the clock," Griff says, slinging an arm around his wife.

"C'mon," Alabama says, handing her a glass of wine. "There. You took the wine. Now you're our guest. Let's party."

Griff runs a broad hand through his hair. "You need to sit down or somethin'?"

Lacey stifles a laugh. "I'm fine, Griff, thank you," she says, warmed by his concern.

"You heard the man." A bright drawl sounds to her left. "Take a load off."

Lacey turns, smiling at Emmy Lou. The southern blond is beatific, her hands on the high swell of her belly. Then she's throwing her arms around Lacey's neck. "I haven't seen you in forever, sugar!"

Lacey returns the hug, then pulls back to eye Emmy Lou's belly. "I still can't believe you're having twins."

Jace's smile is proud. "I can't either."

Emmy Lou wiggles her brows. "Runs in the family."

"Don't know if Jace is ready to handle three girls in the house," Luke drawls, appearing behind them, Sal's hand in his.

Sal laughs. Then she looks at Lacey. "The party's gorgeous, Lace. You did a great job."

"She did," a deep voice rumbles.

Lacey turns to see Seth, wrapping a steady arm around her waist. "Hi," she says, instantly feeling safer at his comforting touch.

"Hey." Seth gives her a crooked grin and her stomach tilts.

They all gather around the large island. Alabama lifts a brow, makes a face of consternation. "Lord, I think I invited half of Nashville."

Lacey appraises the room. "I should be out there slinging business cards."

"Not tonight you ain't," Seth says with a serious look on his face. He pulls her closer, burying his mouth against her ear. "Fun, remember?"

She turns her face, meeting his lips. "In that case," she murmurs against his mouth, "I need more wine."

Luke brushes past her. "I got it, Lace."

Lacey smiles. "It's okay, Luke."

He waves her off, takes everyone's drink orders, and heads in the direction of the bar.

"House is finally done," Jace says to Griff. "How do you feel?"

Griff lifts his bottle of whiskey. "Like we're 'bout to get stupid up in here."

Cheeks flushed pink, Alabama giggles. "Lord, pass the ammunition."

"And by ammunition you mean whiskey," Lacey says.

A roar of laughter goes up and Lacey presses fingertips against the smile on her lips.

Tonight is for fun. For forgetting about her surgery, about her cancer, and spending time with her friends and family. No pity or sorrow in anyone's eyes, just support and love. As the music from the live band swells, she memorizes their faces, their smiles, their laughter, Seth's strong arm around her waist, and she doesn't want this perfect moment to end.

Ever.

He wants to watch her.

His hurricane girl.

Content to wallow in his own misery, Seth stands on the back porch, peeling the label off his bottle of Bud, eyes on the party happening inside. Lacey's dancing with Sal. The group of girls all doing the running man and screaming with laughter. Seeing her so damn happy, too damn gorgeous for words, has his heart in a vise. In a short black dress, her hair waved long around her shoulders, Lacey's got that California glow she's been missing. She's happy. She's smiling, when he hasn't seen a smile out of her in days.

Earlier tonight back at the apartment, she felt so small, so fragile in his arms. All he wanted to do was keep her there, keep her home. But he can't. He can't rope Lacey because he's scared.

Something was on her mind. He could see it.

He wants her to talk to him, to tell him what's wrong, but ever since he punched that goddamn wall, it feels like he punched a hole in their relationship. He saw it in her eyes the second Luke dragged him inside. They were doing okay and then he fucked shit up. He scared her. Showed her he couldn't handle it. And Lacey closed up, worrying about him, when she should be worrying about herself.

Christ, he's a fucking idiot.

With a soft whoosh, the sliding back door opens. Griff Greyson steps onto the porch, into the chilly night air, the clink of his rings on the amber bottle he holds. "Brought you some whiskey."

Seth arches a brow. "Bottom shelf?"

Griff chuckles. "Fuck you." Then, "Bottle or glass?" he asks like he knows where Seth's mind has gone.

"Bottle."

Griff hands it over.

"It's a great party, man," Seth says to Griff, shifting his stance on the porch railing he leans back against. "House is somethin' else too."

"Glad y'all could make it."

Seth takes a swig of the whiskey. "Wouldn't miss it."

Griff eyes the bandage on his hand. "How you doin'? With—" He cuts off, swears, slaps the thighs of his jeans. "Shit. I don't know how to do this." He shakes his head, looking at Seth. "I'm sorry about Lacey, man."

Seth smears a hand across his face, the grit on his jaw. "I can't make her okay and it kills me. I can't fuckin' do a goddamn thing."

Sorrow softens Griff's rugged face. "That's gotta be scary as hell." His throat works, his eyes finding his wife amidst the party guests. The flash of Alabama's red hair like a beacon to the man's gaze. "If it was Al . . . I'd be a fuckin' mess."

"I am."

Griff shoves his hands into his pockets. "Whatever you and California need, you got it."

"I just . . . I just don't fuckin' get it." Seth spits his words, unable to hold back. Like this happy goddamn night wants him to break. "Why Lacey? Why her?"

The door opens. Luke and Jace exit the house, beers in their hands. They exchange looks of concern with Griff, then settle in a loose circle around Seth.

Seth releases a frustrated exhale and takes another long swig of whiskey. "Why's it gotta be Lacey? Why's it gotta be any of us? It's bullshit." He straightens up, rips a hand through his hair, paces the porch. "We've had so much bullshit these last three fuckin' years." Seth roves his eyes to Luke. "You losin' Sal." To Griff. "Alabama gettin' hurt." Now Jace. "And you and Emmy Lou goin' through so much shit, and now Lacey could—"

He cuts off as Lacey passes by the sliding glass door.

Lacey happy, laughing, pulling Sal along with her to the bar, breaks something in Seth.

He turns away, unable to finish the sentence. His vision blurs as hot tears cloud his thoughts.

*Lacey could die.*

The thought's like organ failure, total body and mind shutdown.

"Oh fuck." Seth presses palms into his wet eyes. He doesn't want to cry. He doesn't want to break down, but his boys gather around him. Silent. Steady. Telling him it's okay if he does. Telling him they're here.

"Let it out, man," Jace says.

A shaky shudder rips out of Seth. "She's only thirty. She's too young. She doesn't deserve any of this."

Luke holds his stare. "She doesn't. And you don't."

"I can't lose her." Seth grips the neck of the whiskey bottle and looks out at the sky. "She's gotta be okay. She has to be."

Because if she's not okay, Seth doesn't want to be.

"You ain't losin' her. You're gonna get married and life's gonna work out." Luke wipes his own eyes and grabs Seth's arm. "It's gonna work out. We got you."

Throat bobbing hard, Griff tilts his beer.

Jace nods. "Always, man."

Seth wipes his eyes. The words, the reassurances from his brother, from his friends, are like a balm. His chest, his heart, feels looser than it's been in a long time. Seth exhales. Lifting the whiskey bottle to his eyeline, he says, "Wasn't plannin' to cry after just one drink, but here we are."

With a snort, Griff jerks his head toward the house. "C'mon. You need somethin' to take your mind off this shit."

Seth grins. "More whiskey?"

"Nah," Jace says. "Somethin' better."

"Somethin' stronger." Luke grins, slings an arm around his brother's shoulder. "Music."

# *chapter* TEN

THE NIGHT'S A BLUR OF DRINKING AND DANCING, OF music and laughter, especially when the Brothers Kincaid and Griff take the stage. Despite Seth's hand, they play long and loud into the night. Finally, around midnight the guests slowly trickle out, leaving only their core group remaining. They sit curled up on the L-shaped leather couch, the slider doors thrown open, the buzz of the night outside.

Sal sinks onto Luke's lap, her eyes bright yet tired. "I don't think I've been up this late since Vegas."

"Face it," Jace chuckles, a cold beer in his hand. "We're old."

Emmy Lou yawns, rubbing her stomach. "We're pregnant."

"Still, you danced your ass off," Alabama adds. There's glitter in her hair.

Emmy Lou flaps her arms. "Gotta get that funky chicken down right."

"For the kids," Jace adds, and everyone laughs.

Lacey, sitting beside Seth, stares up at his handsome face as he laughs right along with everyone. Carefree. Happy.

Not like earlier tonight. She had seen him on the front porch with the boys, his posture stiff. And his face—pained.

So much pain.

She knows him well enough to understand he's dealing with it in his own Seth way—torturing himself about something only he knows—but that doesn't mean she won't talk to him about it later.

"Having fun?" she whispers, palming his cheek.

He tugs her closer. Kisses her. "Damn right."

She smiles and settles back. She's a little drunk and it feels great.

"That reminds me of Centennial Park," Luke says to the group, gesturing toward the fiddle on the ground. "The funky chicken."

Seth groans and puts a hand out like he can block Luke's words. "Don't you fuckin' dare, man."

Luke laughs. Even Jace is smirking.

Griff throws his arm around Alabama. "Now you gotta talk, Kincaid."

"Yes," Lacey says, eagerly leaning forward. "Talk."

Jace says, "This is early, like Stonehenge Brothers Kincaid."

Luke, wiggling his dark brows at a glowering Seth, smiles. "We had just started out buskin' and we had camped out at Centennial Park, thinkin' we'd impress everyone headed to the Parthenon. I'd call this our beggin'-for-money-on-a-street-corner career, so you know . . ."

Jace snorts. "There was ten people there and we thought we had made it."

"But Seth wanted more," Luke says. "So he decided to do something about it."

"Yeah. And I did." Seth swears and scoots to the edge of the couch. "Now I'm gonna tell the fuckin' story, man." His eyes swivel around the group. "I was sick of singin' to the same five damn people, so I rented a costume."

Sal's lips twitch. "What kind of costume?"

"A chicken costume," Jace says.

Lacey gasps. "You've dressed as poultry and you've never told me about it?"

"Hey, I just really didn't want to go back to Johnson County," Seth says with a cocky grin.

"So we're in the middle of a set, no idea where our fiddle player had up and gone, when this goddamn chicken strolls up. It was white with this red beak and these molting feathers, but the best part was his cowboy hat." Luke busts out a laugh, causing Sal to rock on his lap.

"Yeah, we could tell it was Seth from the glower," Jace adds.

"I was in there for like half an hour," Seth grouses. "It was goddamn hot."

Luke lifts his beer. "Anyway, Seth starts dancin', fiddlin' while doin' this funky chicken type dance. And we maybe get through three songs before the cops show up."

A groan goes up from Griff and Alabama.

Emmy Lou squeals. "Busted." Turning, she punches Jace in the shoulder. "How on earth have I never heard about this?"

Jace pulls her to him. "Deepest darkest secrets, honey."

"So the cops come over, hasslin' us, threatenin' to charge us with disturbin' the peace."

Seth rolls his eyes. "Like they ain't got nothin' better to do."

"So what happened?" Sal asks.

Luke takes a sip of beer and says, "Seth got us out of it by charmin' the female cop with a fake name and a phone number. They ripped up the ticket then and there."

Lacey laughs. "What was it? The fake name."

Sal leans forward on Luke's lap. "That's what I want to know too."

Thinking on it, Jace holds up a finger. "Somethin' with a T, wasn't it?"

"Tyson," Seth says, kicking his boot up on his knee. "Tyson Feathers."

Alabama gasps. "Oh Lord, you didn't."

"Tell her about the date with the cop," Jace says. "That's the best part."

Seth glares at Jace, but there's laughter in his eyes. "Listen," he says to Lacey, his handsome face pained. "I was forced into it, okay? I ain't responsible for the actions of an eighteen-year-old Seth when we were just down-on-our-luck country boys. The girl literally begged me to go out with her."

A snort from Griff.

"Uh-huh," Lacey says, her expression stern as she tries to keep herself from laughing. Her lips twitch. It's no secret that Seth was a playboy back in the day.

"I take her on this date, some dive Mexican restaurant in Nashville, have a few margaritas, make small talk, and after . . ." A guilty expression sweeps over Seth's face, his eyes flicking to Lacey, and he clears his throat. "She wanted to go back to her place. But only if . . ."

Jace already has his hand over his face, cackling.

Eyes glowing eagerly, Emmy Lou leans forward. "If what? C'mon, sugar, spill it."

Seth's cheeks flame red. Then he says, "Only if I still had the chicken costume."

"No!" Sal gasps and Alabama lets out a scream of laughter.

"Man, fuck y'all," Seth laughs as Luke and Griff crow mercilessly.

Luke slaps his knee. "We made twenty bucks that day and were in the red for two damn months because of that costume, but the real prize was seeing Seth dressed as a chicken."

Seth holds up his middle finger, but he's laughing. "Worth every dime I spent."

The room erupts into laughter. Lacey holds her stomach, the happy sensation going straight to her soul. She's never laughed as hard as she has tonight.

She doesn't want this night to end.

Only as her gaze drifts to her friends, to her family, the weight of reality settles, throwing her off balance.

But it will end.

In ten days, she'll have her surgery. Then radiation. Drugs with side effects.

Her life will change.

Good, bad, it will never be the same.

Her eyes drop to the bandage on Seth's hand.

Not herself, not Seth. Nothing.

Suddenly, everything feels too heavy. Her worries bubble up like a dark cloud thwarting her blue skies.

She's never been this scared, because she has everything to lose.

Everything she's worked so hard for in her life. Gone. It could be gone. Her business. Her health. Seth.

Tears fill her eyes.

"Excuse me," she whispers, getting off the couch.

At the island, she refills her glass with champagne, but she doesn't drink it, only watches the bubbles climb to the top. Feeling faint, she presses a hand against the cool marble to collect her whirlwind of thoughts.

What if it's worse than the doctor thinks? Oh God. What if they open her up and it's spread?

She chugs the champagne in one quick gulp.

A burst of laughter has her looking over. The bright, laughing faces of her friends have her feelings welling bitterly. Everyone's so healthy and happy and she has a ticking bomb inside of her. Her eyes drop to Emmy Lou's stomach.

What if she can't have kids?

Ever.

And what if Seth realizes he wants them? She'd be denying him that.

Her eyes move to Seth, bickering with Luke.

What even is their future? Seth watching her get sick? Seth marrying some half-life version of herself isn't what Lacey wants for him. It isn't what she wants for herself.

Worse, what if he regrets it?

What if he leaves?

Her thoughts, her world spins until she goes dizzy.

Only it's not the champagne that has her head swimming. It's doubt. Despair.

Will she be here? In a year, in five, will she be here?

A tear slips down her cheek. She should do the right thing. Wait on the wedding. Give Seth an out. For his own sake. Before it's too late.

Lacey stands still, eyes closed, barely breathing, when she realizes the laughter, the conversation's stopped.

"Lace?" Sal's voice is gentle.

Then, a warm hand on the small of her back. Seth stands tall over her, shielding her from the worried stares of the room.

"One day," he says, so much love in his eyes it leaves her breathless. "This is just one day, ain't it, princess?"

"Yes," she whispers. Her hands wrap around his broad shoulders.

His blue eyes search her face, then, reading her better than anyone ever has, he nods. "Let's go home."

She starts to tell him yes, but before she can, her legs give out.

"I got you." Seth's voice is soft and then he's there, picking her up in his arms.

Clinging to him, Lacey keeps her face burrowed in the curve of his neck. All she hears is the sound of his hard bootsteps over the floorboards, his rumble of a goodbye and murmured whispers from their friends, as he strides for the front door.

Then—the sensation of bright light turning to night, a frosty chill causing her to tremble. But she doesn't care.

She's in Seth's arms and for now, that's good enough.

It's two a.m. by the time Lacey and Seth go to bed.

Seth sits and watches as she changes into a pale pink sleep shirt, love and worry warring in his ocean-blue eyes.

"You looked beautiful tonight."

"I better have looked beautiful tonight because I singlehandedly ruined their party." By now, Lacey's on steadier legs, even though her embarrassment's off the charts. Another party ruined because she couldn't keep it together.

He chuckles. "You did no such thing."

"At least I didn't fall into a lake this time."

Seth's expression turns dark. With a sigh, he unbuttons his shirt and stretches out on the bed. "I ain't laughin', princess."

"Well, I have to laugh, or else I'll just cry." She crawls across the bed toward him. "Although, I still like you carrying me out of parties."

Seth laughs and reaches for her, pulling her into his lap. He kisses her temple, murmurs into her hair, "You're exhausted."

She palms his scruff, curls up against his broad chest. "You are too."

"Yeah, but I ain't runnin' on fumes, Lace." He shakes his head. "The party was a bad idea."

"No, Seth. It wasn't. I needed that. I needed to laugh tonight." She looks up at him, and the hard clench of his jaw tells her he's blaming himself. "I just . . . I got too inside my mind. And I started thinking . . ."

"'Bout what?"

"About the wedding."

She feels his entire body tense. "What about it?"

Lacey stares at Seth, all her doubts, all her worries on the tip of her tongue. But how to say it? She'd hurt him. Her eyes fall to his bandaged hand. But if she goes through with this wedding, will she hurt him even more?

"Lace?"

His blue eyes search hers and she sees he's afraid. Afraid of her answer.

She can't do this to him. Hurt him like this. It's like digging out her own heart with a pickaxe.

Her eyes shutter.

She can be strong.

So, swallowing down her worries, burying her anxiety, she forces a smile and gives a little shrug. "I was thinking we go with lobster instead of beef."

His throat works as he stares at her, deciding whether to believe her. "Lobster instead of beef, huh? You sure that's all it was?"

"Positive."

For a long moment, he says nothing, his eyes never once leaving her face. Then, he exhales, tightening his hold on her. "Should I be worried?"

She thinks of the invites buried in her bag. "No." A lie.

Seth smiles sadly. "You know I'm only ever going to love you, right?" His voice is thick. Low. "I love you, Lacey. So don't run from me. Don't."

A tear slips down her cheek. Lacey stares up at Seth, transfixed. His strong jaw, the love in his eyes, the strength in his words—it's all she can do not to fall apart.

Seth, this wonderful man, who always dragged Lacey back from the dark places her mind would go, who's always there for her when she's falling apart, is here. Ready and willing to hold whatever she wants to give.

And she wants to, God, how she aches to. Wants to explode from her heart and scream her worries, her fears, her anxieties, but she can't.

Because saying it breaks them.

And she doesn't want to break them. They were already broken, a long time ago, and now they've come together, heart to heart and soul to soul.

That is them. Her and Seth. Burning together, until the end.

"I love you too," she says, lifting her eyes to meet his steadfast gaze. "And I'll try, okay? I'll try hard not to run."

Seth runs a tan hand down her arm, slowly lowering the strap of her bra. "Don't push me away, princess."

Her heart thunders, and breathlessly, she whispers, "I won't."

Lowering her gently into the pillows, he presses his lips to her throat. "You sure?"

"Yes," she gasps, her voice hoarse with anticipation.

"How sure?" he asks, raising a wicked brow. Lacey drags her nails down his shoulders, but he grabs her wrists to bring them high above her.

She moans, arches beneath him. "So sure."

Slowly, in a way that's holy and pure and reverent, Seth begins to kiss his way down her body. Her panties disappear. The hot pulse of his breath as his mouth sweeps across the inside of her thigh.

And Lacey falls away.

Worries, woe—everything bad gone in this instant.

There's only the good.

Her and Seth.

Their future.

# *chapter* ELEVEN

THE NEXT AFTERNOON, LACEY SITS IN THE PARKING LOT of Bluegrass Bakery, waiting on Seth. They've agreed to meet here after his practice to finally pick their cake design and flavor. And she can't wait.

In fact, she feels steadier than she's felt since her diagnosis.

One day at a time. One breath. One heartbeat. They take it all at one time.

They take it together.

Seth's calming words have lingered all morning. They've helped her regroup. But that's Seth. Her rock in the face of a storm.

She couldn't do this without him. She doesn't want to.

Though she had tentatively broached the subject of possibly postponing the wedding, she held back her true worries. That Seth will marry a woman he doesn't deserve. That she isn't being strong enough for him. That she doesn't want him to settle.

Instead, like always, she buried it deep.

She'll get through this. She can do it. Just nine days to go until her surgery.

And while she waits, she'll work.

Inhaling a steeling breath, Lacey taps out a run-of-show schedule on her laptop. Best to get in as much work as she can before her surgery. She'll be out of commission for at least a week, and God knows Seth isn't going to let her work.

She chuckles at the thought, loving him.

*Fuck work,* she suddenly thinks and straightens up.

Instead, she pulls her wedding planner onto her lap. Her lips curve as she flips past her dresses to the tux Seth's selected. He'll look so handsome. So sexy. A laugh bubbles off her lips. He'll look better than her.

Resolve fills her.

She and Seth—they'll have their life. It'll just be a little less planned and a little more chaotic, but they're good at that.

After all, it's how they got here, isn't it? One unexpected hookup and now she's got Seth Kincaid's ring on her finger. She laughs again. Who would have thought?

A ping on her phone.

Lacey checks, expecting a deposit from a new client; instead she finds a news alert in her email about the Brothers Kincaid.

Protective instincts have her bristling. Stupid *Star*. Damn trashy tabloid has done everything they can to libel their boys. She can already see Emmy Lou picking up the phone to give them a piece of her mind.

But as Lacey clicks the link, she sees the story isn't about the Brothers Kincaid.

It's about her.

Her eyes pop open, the headline like a knife to her back.

*From I Dos to Deathbed? What Are Seth Kincaid and His Future Bride Hiding?*

No. Oh no.

It's not true. But it could be.

It's close.

Too close.

A guttural cry shakes out of her. Her hands tremble, bile builds in her throat as she reads the article. She wants to puke. Puke all over her wedding plans, her cancer, her life.

Another ping.

Sal: *Lacey, can you call me?*

The lump in her throat grows.

*Ping.*

Alabama: *Are you okay?*

*Breathe in. Breathe out.*

Lacey stares at the white shutters of the bakery, the happy dancing cupcake illustrations, and her vision blurs.

"It's cake," she whispers.

It's just cake.

Not making important decisions that could ruin another person's life.

A rush of hot tears fill her eyes. She can't do this anymore.

She doesn't *want* to do this anymore.

The light, the hope, flickers in her heart.

Extinguishes.

With a gasp, she puts the car in gear and peels out of the parking lot.

She needs to get away from her own heartbeat, from the wild racing of her mind.

*Get away. Get away.*

Anywhere.

The sex last night wrecked his goddamn world.

Late-afternoon sun in his rearview, Seth rolls his Bronco up to the curb of Bluegrass Bakery, the memory of Lacey sleeping easy and gentle in his arms this morning fresh in his mind. She was so goddamn beautiful he would have been content saying fuck it all and staying in bed with her the rest of his life.

Because that's what he's giving. And that's what she's getting. No doubt.

Still, last night eats at him. She looked unsteady at Griff and Alabama's party. He didn't miss the current of worry in her green eyes. He got the feeling she wasn't telling him everything. And so, he did all he could do to reassure her that he loves her. He knows it ain't a magic fix—he knows her pain and worry won't go away overnight, but if he can make her feel loved and safe and supported, it's all he wants.

He frowns as he approaches the front of the bakery. Lacey's

perky little VW is nowhere to be seen. When it comes to everything else in life—shopping, tours, Sunday suppers—she's late. But when it comes to parties, her job, she's like clockwork.

As he enters the bakery, Seth's instantly hit by the aroma of dough and sugar. With the jingle of the door chimes comes a small woman with long gray hair from the kitchen.

"Help you, darlin'?"

"I'm lookin' for a girl," he drawls. "Blond. Beautiful."

"Let me guess, you're marryin' her."

"Damn right I am."

The woman dusts her floured hands off on her apron. "Well, lover boy, the girl of your dreams hasn't been in yet. If you have a seat, I'll get together some samples while you wait."

Chuckling, Seth nods and takes a seat at a bubblegum-pink table.

He hasn't been there a minute before his phone buzzes.

Sal, not Lacey.

"Seth." Sal sounds breathless. "Are you with Lacey?"

"No. We're meetin' at the bakery. Why?"

She swears. "Have you seen the *Star*?"

He bristles, already shoving out of his chair and bolting forward for the front door. Something's wrong.

Something bad.

"What's goin' on, Sal?"

"The article's awful," Sal says, her voice burning with uncharacteristic anger. Fear. "She won't answer my calls. You have to find her, Seth."

"Shit. I'll call you back." Heart thundering, Seth hangs up and checks the website.

He freezes on the spot. The headline turns his blood to ice.

"Mother*fuckers*," he snarls, not recognizing his own voice. His fists curl at his side, jaw clenching so hard he could break a tooth.

What the fuck the *Star* was thinking publishing a story like this is beyond Seth, but he already knows one thing. He's gonna ruin that woman at the *Star*, and while Seth would love nothing better than to wage nuclear war, first, he's gotta find Lacey.

He's gotta find his girl.

He presses the phone to his ear, his heart dangerously close to its last beat as he listens to it ring. "Pick up, princess. Pick up."

But her phone goes straight to voice mail.

He swears and breaks into a run. Then he's in the Bronco, burning asphalt, moving so goddamn fast he could make can make the old car fly.

*Please, Lacey. Be there. Be at home.*

She's not at home.

By now, the pink and orange of the earlier sunset has been painted over with black. Arms crossed, Seth stands at the large window of his loft and stares out over the river. Worrying, waiting on Lacey.

"Where would she go?" Sal asks. She's perched on the edge of the couch, a wriggling Cash in her arms.

"I don't know." Seth rips a hand through his hair. His pulse rages like a wildfire in his veins.

They've spent the last three hours driving around Nashville and camped out at the apartment in the hopes that she'd come back.

He knows one thing, though. She's not missing. She took off. She's scared and she doesn't feel safe.

Luke hangs up the phone. "Griff and Al haven't heard from her either. They're gonna head out, drive around."

His brother's face is anguished, taking on Seth's pain. No doubt flashing back to when Sal was kidnapped by some lunatic at the hospital. Luke's worst nightmare—and Seth's slowly getting there himself.

The longer he's gone without hearing from Lacey, the more dread has curdled his stomach.

"Fuck." Seth manages to move, to uproot his feet from the spot and pace. He rubs at the building ache in his chest. His girl is scared. That article broke her. All the emotions she's been trying so hard to bottle up, unleashed, and now she's in defense mode.

Flight.

Seth plows a hand through his hair. Twists it. "I shouldn't have left her today," he says, more to himself than the room, but Sal and Luke look up. The devil in his head has him blaming himself.

"This is my fault," he says, guilt lashing his voice. "She was tryin' to talk to me last night, but I didn't listen. I was tryin' to fix it as fuckin' usual."

"Was it about the wedding?" Sal asks, letting Cash loose. The baby toddles across the room.

Seth stops pacing for a moment and looks at Sal.

The tone of her voice—she knows something.

"Sal, tell me what the hell's goin' on."

Sal hesitates for a few seconds, then flattens her lips. "She never mailed the invites." Tears fill her eyes. Luke, sitting beside her, rubs her back in slow circles. "She wanted to talk to you, but didn't want to worry you. She thinks you're getting into something you'll regret. That you'll leave. That you'll want an out."

There's a pause, and then Sal looks down, swiping at her eyes.

Seth stares, his world rocked. The static in his head building. An out? A goddamn out?

He had no idea Lacey was worrying about him. He thought she was worried about the stress, her cancer, her career. Never once did he imagine she had doubts about him.

Christ.

He's an asshole.

She tried to tell him. Maybe not outright, but she had tried. Broached the subject hesitantly to feel him out. And what did he do? He tried to fix it instead of just fucking listening to her. And why? Because he was terrified of what she was going to say. Because he couldn't stand to see her sad, not for one goddamn second.

He thought he had reassured her last night, but all he did was inadvertently force her to bury her fears. He didn't know how deep her worries had roots. But after everything she's been through, of fucking course she'd worry. Her mother went through cancer only to be abandoned by her husband. He should have seen it. How she was trying to be strong for the both of them, despite all the pain the past triggered for her.

And this *Nashville Star* article was the last straw of it all.

All her what-ifs made real in black and white.

Seth lets out a harsh breath. His chest caves in on itself, crushing him. His air. His heart. Lacey is out there somewhere.

Alone. Vulnerable. Scared.

Where would she go? What if she got into an accident? Images of Lacey, hurt, on the side of the road, flash through his mind.

Christ. If anything happens to her, he'll kill that woman at the *Star*. He'll burn down their goddamn world and then light himself on fire next.

"Cash." Luke's low drawl takes Seth from his grim thoughts. Seth glances over. Cash coos as he approaches the coffee table, slapping his chubby hands on the wood, the stack of papers, Lacey's wedding magazines.

A ping on Luke's phone. He exhales. "Jace ain't seen her. Shit." He leans back on the couch, looking as frustrated as Seth feels. "Where the hell would she go?"

Skirting the edge of insanity, Seth tips his gaze down and shakes his head. There's a loud burst of bubbly laughter as Cash swipes the papers off the table and onto the ground.

They land faceup. Architectural brochures. Farmhouses sketched on fields of country land.

*Their* land.

Realization dawns.

A memory from weeks ago. What could be a lifetime.

*I feel safe here. Like I could come to this spot when everything's wrong and somehow it would all be okay.*

Heart pumping hard, Seth sinks into a crouch next to Cash. He stares at the farmhouse sketches. Then he ruffles Cash's dark hair and grins at the wild, jubilant cry his nephew lets out.

"You found her too, huh, kid?"

# chapter TWELVE

LACEY SIGHS AND DRAWS HER LEGS INTO HER CHEST, resting her cheek on her knees. She lets the silence of the country surround her. The stars above wink like bright SOS signals. No phones. No noise. Just her and her thoughts. Which is probably a bad idea. The worst.

At the sound of movement, the flash of a light, Lacey looks up. A shadow darkens her eyeline. Tall. Muscular. A deep rumble of a voice. "What're you doin', princess?"

She sniffs. "Being sad."

Seth waves a flashlight. "I can see that. I can also see that you're freezin' to death out here."

She lifts her chin. "I've been colder."

"I know you have. Tonight, you ain't gotta be."

A blanket's slipped around her shoulders. Then Seth's sitting beside her on the dewy ground, the flashlight casting a slow ripple of light as he sets it down. Heat rolls off his body, warming her. A gigantic sigh heaves out of him as he leans back against the tree she's been using as support. "You scared me to death, you know."

"I know. I'm sorry."

A slow shake of his head. "That article, Lace. I'm the one who's sorry."

"It's not your fault," she whispers. "It freaked me out."

"Me too." He takes her shoulder, gently turning her toward him. "But no more, princess. You can't do that to me. You can't run off like that. I damn near had a heart attack."

She rests her head on his shoulder.

A country quiet falls. Crickets. The rush of the river.

Seth's deep drawl breaks the silence. "Sal says you never mailed invites."

Lacey sighs and lifts her face. "She shouldn't have told you that."

"Yes, she should've." Seth's eyes search hers. "Because I didn't hear what you were sayin', really sayin', and hell, that's on me." He swears. "I shoulda listened better when you said you were stressed. I was just so damn scared of you pullin' away from me I wasn't gonna let you."

Lacey tucks herself closer. "Everything feels so big right now. Like our entire next year literally blew up."

"I know." Seth hesitates, then asks, "Do you not want to marry me?"

She stares, aghast, hating herself for the tortured look in his eyes. "Seth, no." She shakes her head. "I still want you. I want everything with you. I'm just afraid. I'm so afraid we'll never get it. That *I'll* never get it."

She inhales and like a switch is flipped, all her pent-up worry, her doubt, streams out like a hot lava flow. "It's not fair to you. What if in a year it comes back? What if they have to cut off my breasts? What if I die?" Seth's wince is anguished. "What if I can't give you a family? I mean, I'm the selfish one taking that away from you. You didn't sign up for any of this."

Seth chuckles. A slow roll of a deep rumble that curls her stomach. "This is exactly what I signed up for. This. Our life. Together, Lacey." He tugs her close. "It ain't all gonna be easy, but damn if I'm doin' it with anyone else."

"Seth . . ."

"Don't try to talk me out of it, princess. You're stuck with me." Seth traces a finger over her cheekbone and lays his mouth beside her ear. "And I ain't leavin' you. You hear me? I will never leave you." Gripping her shoulders, he pulls back to look at her, unshed tears in his eyes. "You are the love of my life, Lace, and I will never have another. You gotta know that."

His words break her. Her face crumples, only Seth has her. She weeps in his arms, her tears soaking the front of his shirt. Catharsis. A release of everything she's been holding in, pushing down.

A sob escapes Seth and his arms tighten around her waist. "I don't think you understand how much I can't live without you. I don't think you realize how much nothing can happen to you."

With that, he lifts her into his arms, and, still sitting, she wraps her legs around his waist. The back of his hand cradles her head protectively as she burrows her face in his neck. She inhales his Seth-scent and goes back in time, in her memory. To Los Angeles, to whiskey, to Smoky Mountains and secret kissing, and dive bar dance floors.

The two of them sit together in the crisp air, holding each other, clinging tight, shaking. Lacey nestles deeper into Seth's body, resting her cheek on his shoulder.

"I'm sorry I'm not braver," she murmurs.

"Lace, baby, you ain't gotta be brave. You just gotta be here." He pulls the blanket around her shoulders to keep her warm. "One day at a time, remember?"

"I remember."

"'Sides, you ain't supposed to save me from this. I'm supposed to save you."

She sits up to look at him. His handsome face contorted in grief. She cups the side of his strong jaw. "Maybe we save each other."

"You already did that. So many times, princess, you pulled me from the brink of all my bullshit. And now, I've got you."

She smiles through her tears. "Why do you wrangle me?"

He kisses her. "Because you're worth the wrangle." Adjusting her in his arms, Seth pulls her down into his lap. "I ain't sure what the future holds. But I do know one thing. It's you and me."

She stares at him, at this man she loves with her entire soul, her protector of the highest order, and her chest feels heavy. "I love you, Seth. Too much." Fresh tears fill her eyes. "And I'm sorry for pushing you away."

He chuckles. "Like I was goin' anywhere anyway."

They relax into each other, stretching out on the damp grass. Lacey's hand tangles with Seth's, fingers locking.

She smiles. "I could stay out here forever."

"That's the plan, princess." He lifts a hand, points a finger. "See that sky? That's ours. We're gonna build our house, and we're gonna sing whatever damn song we want."

"Hmm. I like that."

Tilting her face, she scours the stars, the milky night sky. Cradled against Seth's broad chest, his arms wrapped around her, there are no more unanswered questions or hard doubts. There is this moment, right here, right now. Life is short. And all she can do is live. One step, one day, one breath, one heart-beat at a time.

Starting with Seth.

All she wants is him. Not a house or an expensive wedding, just Seth and her health.

Those two things are her most important focus.

"Seth," she ventures, looking into his piercing blue eyes. "About the wedding . . ."

He cuts her off with a shake of his head. "If you want to wait, let's do it. I don't want you worryin' about a damn thing." His voice is pained, choked. Like he hates the idea, is dying over it, but he'll give it to her. It makes her love him even more.

"I don't want to have a wedding," Lacey says, her heart content with her decision. "I just want you. I want to marry you, Seth."

"Are you sure?" His expression is sad, thoughtful. "You've worked so hard. I ain't takin' this away from you."

"So sure. I want to be your wife." At that, Seth's handsome face softens. She leans in, their mouths colliding, Seth's kiss like the best kind of whiskey. Smooth and honeyed.

"Let's go to the courthouse," she says, suddenly aching to say their vows. "Tomorrow."

He chuckles, cups her face. "Nah. We ain't doin' that."

Her eyes widen. "Then what?"

He grins, then kisses her. "I think I got a better idea."

# chapter THIRTEEN

THE NEXT AFTERNOON, THE DOOR TO TONK'S SWINGS open. Dusty floorboards rattle with the motion of boots and heels. Luke leads the pack, followed by Sal and the rest of their friends. They stop and stare at the setup.

One long rustic table covered with vases of simple wildflower arrangements. A keg waits to be tapped. Behind the bar, a bartender arranges bottles of champagne. Neon glows bright on the wall. The jukebox pumps out a carefully crafted selection of country tunes.

Everyone looks confused. And they should be.

Last night, after Seth and Lacey got home from the farm, they had put a plan together and then sent out a cryptic text.

No more fear. Only living.

"Hey, y'all look ready to party," Seth says, leaning against the wall.

Luke, adjusting a babbling Cash in his arms, gives his brother a look. "What're we doin' here, Seth?"

Seth throws him a wicked grin. "We're havin' a party."

Sal's green eyes glint. "What kind of party?"

"The best kind," a soft voice says.

The room explodes with whistles and cheers as Lacey exits the backroom. Alabama gasps and grabs Sal's arm.

"Y'all are gettin' married!" Emmy Lou shrieks, jumping up and down, her golden curls bouncing.

Lacey beams and smooths a hand down the front of the light pink satin slip dress she wears. "May I present dress number one."

Seth stares. The breath from his lungs, the words from his mouth—gone. His entire universe, his weakness, stands in front of him. He's never seen Lacey look more beautiful, radiant. Here, in their bar, she just shines.

A round of happy laughter and congratulations makes its way around the group. Griff steps up to clap Seth's shoulder and Jace shakes his head.

"Sneaky asshole," Jace says and Seth snorts.

"Goddamn right. Rustled up a preacher and a couple of kegs." Seth gives Lacey a grin. "And she's still gotta make the most dramatic entrance known to man."

Lacey laughs. "This is what I get for letting Seth plan it." She looks at the group, silver lining her eyes, and everyone instantly sobers. She reaches for Seth's hand, drawing him into her. "We didn't want to wait anymore. Life's short and we're taking back our wedding day and making it ours. It's not going to be sad." She smiles. "Besides. This is more like us anyway. Kinda fancy, kinda country."

Seth looks at his friends, clears the knot from his throat. "Tonight, it's our bar. Our damn weddin.'"

"Amen," Alabama says, her gray eyes misty.

Griff lets out a rebel yell. "Hell yes," he whoops, the sound booming off the walls.

Sal goes to her sister and embraces her. "I love that, Lacey."

"Mom and Dad are gonna kill ya," Luke says, but when his eyes meet Seth's, his are teary.

"I know." Seth squeezes Lacey's hand. "But they're gonna have to deal with it."

A clearing of the throat has everyone turning.

The preacher stands there. "Y'all ready to begin the ceremony?"

Lacey jumps and claps her hands together, startling the preacher. "Absolutely not," she says, flustered. "I need to change. I need dress number two."

Seth chuckles, running his palms down her slender shoulders. "Easy, princess. We got time."

"Yeah. We do," she says, smiling soft.

Then with a gasp she snaps into action. The Lacey he knows. This wedding may be simple and easy, but his girl isn't, and he loves that about her.

Lacey turns to Sal, grabs Emmy Lou's and Alabama's hands. "Come help me get ready." Linking arms, the women gather at the bar for glasses of champagne and then, in a torrent of synchronized squealing, head off toward the back room.

Griff returns from the bar with shots of tequila. His tawny eyes glint. "You 'bout to have yourself a good night, Seth."

The men gather round and Seth looks to his brother, to Jace. In Luke's arms, Cash giggles, squirming around in his banjo footie pajamas.

"Raise hell, have some fun," Griff toasts, and with amens, they raise their shots, shoot them back with smooth finesse.

Exhaling, Luke meets his eyes. His brother's face is serious, nostalgic. "Never thought I'd see this damn day."

Seth's eyes move to where Lacey disappeared mere moments ago. "Me either," he murmurs, his heart thundering in his chest at the thought that soon she'll be his wife.

His hands shake. His heartbeat pounds like a kick drum. He's so goddamn nervous his stomach's pinned in his boots.

Hell, he's wanted to marry Lacey ever since he put that ring on her finger. Never thought it would be like this, wearing a plaid shirt, jeans and boots in a dingy dive bar, a handful of guests watching, a jukebox pounding out Hank Williams, but to him, it's perfect.

He hopes this is what Lacey wants. That she doesn't regret it—or him—because he knows he can never work hard enough to deserve her, but goddamn he'll try.

Beside him, Luke nudges his shoulder with his own. A gleam in his eyes. "She's late. Think she climbed out the bathroom window?"

"Cut it out, man," Seth grouses, trying not to check the neon clock on the wall.

Across from him, Sal gives him a smile.

Anxious, he shifts, wiping clammy palms on the legs of his jeans.

Then there's a creak of the floorboard.

A gasp from Sal.

Seth's jaw drops and he finds his breath catching in his throat. Nothing could prepare him for this moment. Lacey looks like a damn goddess. She wears a shimmering floor-length gown with spaghetti straps and a sexy sheer bodice that hugs her flawlessly. The stark white color makes her bronze skin pop and her bright green eyes sparkle. Her long blond hair is loose, curled slightly at the ends. Around her neck she wears the delicate gold locket that was her mother's.

In disbelief, he closes his eyes. Opens them.

And she's still here.

*His.*

*His wife.*

As she walks toward him, Seth inhales a ragged breath. His and Lacey's gazes lock. No nerves in her eyes. Only love and adoration burn within those bright, brilliant green eyes of hers.

Seth's vision blurs, and then Lacey's in front of him, slipping her steady hands into his. She gives them a squeeze and all he can do is shake his head at the fact that this one singular motion, her graceful touch, always has him finding his place. Where he belongs. The strength she gives him is endless.

He never imagined a love like this. A woman like this. Brave. Sexy. Strong. A woman who loves him for who he is. Despite his mistakes, his bullshit, she's stood by him, has had his back with unfailing belief. She's saved him, whipped up his life into something he never thought possible.

And Seth knows one thing is true—he wouldn't last a single day without this woman beside him.

Finally, he finds his voice. "You look beautiful, princess."

Tears fill her eyes. "So do you," she breathes. She tilts her head. "Are you ready?"

In answer, he pulls her close. He ain't playing hands off. Hell nah, not today. "Smartest thing I ever did was put that ring on your hand."

She scoffs. "You got lucky."

He sobers. "I did. Damn lucky." He pins his eyes to hers. He knows the preacher's waiting, but he can't wait. He has to say this. "I'm with you forever, Lacey. Good, bad. Happy, sad. Whatever comes our way, we take it. Together."

Lacey blinks away tears as his words wash over her.

"Rest of my life, until the end of my damn days," Seth says in a steady drawl. "I'll love you."

A loud sob from Emmy Lou.

And as for Alabama, Griff and Jace . . .

The entire room's losing it and they haven't even started yet. Only Cash, held tight in Griff's tattooed arms, squawks his objections.

"You can't do this." Lacey sniffles as she turns to the group. Tears drip onto her bouquet. She doubles over, laughing. "You're gonna make me ruin my makeup."

"Goddamn," Luke says in a hoarse voice, wiping his eyes on his shirt sleeve.

Sal steps forward, helps Lacey straighten up, adjusting her veil, her train. She gives Seth a wobbly smile.

Then Lacey and Seth turn to face the preacher.

One breath.

One heartbeat.

One day at a time.

Starting with today.

# chapter FOURTEEN

LACEY LAUGHS AS SHE WATCHES SETH TAKE A SHOT WITH the guys. His jacket's gone, draped over a chair, leaving him in a plaid long-sleeved shirt that's been shoved up on his forearms. With mussed hair and a mischievous grin, he looks so damn sexy her legs could buckle here and now.

It's been a night, and while she's tired, she doesn't want this magical time to ever end. What's a better way to celebrate their love than being surrounded by their closest friends and family?

After they said their vows, a private chef prepared them a delicious southern meal for dinner, and now everyone's gathered around the bar. Jace plays bartender. Emmy Lou, Alabama and Sal perch on stools.

Seth pounds the bar, says to Jace, "Pour a little more, you stingy bastard. This is a celebration."

Jace arches a solemn brow. "It's your weddin' night, man."

Griff, Cash cradled in his brawny tattooed arms, laughs. "Shit, Seth, that's a gotcha ring if I ever seen one."

"Wouldn't have it any other way," Seth drawls, lifting his hand to flash his silver wedding band.

Alabama scoffs and nods at Griff's bright band of gold. "Like you're one to talk."

Griff gives her a wink and a kiss.

"It looks good on him," Lacey teases, coming up behind Seth. She ducks under his arm and he pulls her close. "But I don't think any of you have complimented my third dress tonight." She waves a hand around her flashy off-white minidress with ostrich feather cuffs.

Seth clicks his tongue. "Pathetic. No one loves her or pays any attention."

Lacey scoffs and holds up a manicured hand. "I can't with him sometimes."

Seth glances at Cash and lifts an impressed brow. "Kid can still hang."

Lacey peers down at her nephew, his dark eyes heavy with sleep. "Barely."

Sal groans and covers her eyes. "Parents of the year right here."

Luke chuckles. "He knows a good party."

Griff jostles Cash. "Ain't nothin' to worry about. He's gettin' some lessons from Uncle Griff."

Luke, choking back a laugh, shakes his head. "Lord, help me."

"It's my turn." Alabama opens her arms and smirks. "Pass the baby, Greyson."

"I'm passin', I'm passin'," Griff grumbles, looking none too pleased to let go of Cash.

Emmy Lou waves a lazy hand, drops it to her heavy belly. "Y'all remember this, and come to my house when these babies are born."

Jace, polishing a glass, chuckles. "I'll need all the backup I can get."

A round of laughs go up. More drinks are poured, the jukebox cranks out Willie Nelson at brain-splitting levels, Cash is finally put to bed in his playpen. The night shows no signs of ending, just beginning.

Lacey locks eyes with Seth in the dim bar light. His grin is enough to power her heart, fuel her soul. Tonight's a celebration. Even with her surgery looming, she has nothing to worry about. Not tonight. She feels overwhelmed, steadied by love, by friendship. Everyone's shown up, gathered around her and Seth to celebrate their special day.

Drunk and happy and in love. The way it should be.

A wave of contentment sweeps over Lacey, and for a brief second, she closes her eyes.

This is how they heal. They let go. Make room for forever.

Because love . . . it never fails.

Seth slugs down his beer, slams the bottle on the bar top. Turns to Lacey. "Let's dance, princess. Put those heels to good use."

Sal, gracefully tipsy, shouts, "Luke, go forth and make music!"

"Hell, you're comin' with me, darlin'." Grinning, Luke picks Sal up in his arms and slings her over his shoulder. Sal squeals and pounds on his back, laughing.

"No sad songs," Seth calls to Luke as his brother hustles to the jukebox. "Not tonight." He looks at Lacey, brushing hair out of her eyes. "Dance with me, princess?"

She nods, her throat tightening unbearably.

Then as a swell of bluegrass floods the room, Seth's swinging her into his arms, pulling her against his broad chest. For a long second, she relishes this moment. Tonk's. Saying their vows in this dingy dive bar they fought in—and then fell in love in—so long ago.

It's her and Seth. Impromptu and flighty and chaotic and so damn perfect she wouldn't trade it for anything.

Seth's deep drawl rumbles out. "You happy, Lace?"

She smiles up at him. "I am."

"You like the wedding? It's what you wanted?" His worried eyes search hers, making sure she's happy. Always giving her everything she needs and then some.

"It was everything, Seth."

She kisses him, then leans back to take him in. Her heart tightens to the point of pain. He looks so damn handsome. She cups his cheek, holds his eyes. "I wouldn't change a thing."

Nothing. Her wedding was beautiful and beyond what she ever could have imagined. And his vows. She'll never find words to describe what Seth's vows did to her. The way his jaw trembled, the fierceness of his words. She heard so much even if he never said it.

*I'll never leave you. You're safe, you're mine. I've got you.*

*Forever.*

Suddenly it hits her. She grabs his arm, stilling their slow sway, and gasps. "Seth. You're my husband. We're *married*."

*Husband.*

The word thrills her.

His eyes flash. "We are. No gettin' away now. You're stuck with me, princess."

"Good," she says, gripping his shirt. "I wanna be stuck on you." He gives her a twirl and when she comes back to him, she says, "Lacey Kincaid, that has a nice ring to it."

Pride in his eyes, he gives a deep, joyous laugh, the sound curling her stomach, echoing around the bar.

To think she almost lost sight of Seth. Let the roughness of the last few weeks steal her joy. Her hope. Well, not anymore. Because there is nothing she and Seth can't do. Getting better, beating cancer, is just one of many feats they'll tackle in this long run of life together.

As Lacey sways, Seth's hungry gaze follows her, his eyes, his arms eating her up. "You look beautiful tonight," he whispers, his deep voice like velvet unfurling around her, and she shivers.

He kisses her throat, her lips. His hands roam over her body, her hips, waist, breasts. And it's like an explosion. It's more than she can take.

"We need to get a room," she hisses as she leans into him.

"Believe me, I got one." Tugging her close, he nips at her throat and her nipples tighten in response. "We sneak out after we cut the fuckin' cake."

"After cake," she echoes. Heat rushes her, her stomach curling in anticipation. She wants Seth. All over her body. Buried inside her.

Becoming one, forever.

Because whatever comes next, they take that on too.

Together.

Seth, Lacey in his arms, slams into their hotel room. She squeals at the massive suite, the bucket of champagne on the entry table, takes a deep inhale of his woodsy scent, kisses him, and then he's setting her on her feet. "Easy, princess," he says with a chuckle, watching as she wobbles once in her high heels, then spins herself across to the room to collapse on the foot of the bed.

She looks up at him, her messy blond hair obscuring her face. "Weddings are exhausting."

He gives her a grin. "Good thing you're only havin' one."

She giggles. "Good thing."

She's drunk. Adorable. Beautiful beyond words. Hell, who can blame her? He's already there himself. High on Lacey's I-do kiss.

He's whipped and he wouldn't have it any other way.

A rush of emotions crashes over him as he stares at his girl.

*His wife.*

*His goddamn wife.*

Every second of tonight was pure fucking heaven.

Without words, Seth dims the lights and Lacey's eyes turn heavy-lidded. The delicate gold locket around her neck glows in the shadows. Slipping off the bed, she comes to him.

Seth toes off his boots while Lacey's graceful hands rove up his shirt. Lust blazes across her beautiful face as she slides a slender leg between his crotch. Her voice a breathless whisper. "I need you, Seth."

"I know." He runs his palms up her hips. Her waist, her curves feel like silk beneath his palms. "Oh, we gonna take our time tonight."

"Are we?" One of her eyebrows arches. Haughty. Confident. So damn sexy. Seth lets out a growl as his dick swells in his jeans.

"We are."

Slowly, he peels her thin dress from her body, watching feathers from her cuffs dance around the room. Then his brain proceeds to melt down when he sees what she's got on underneath. The tiniest bra and a lace thong that shows off her toned ass.

He gapes at her. Jesus Christ. She's gonna make a sinner out of him.

"You been wearin' that all night and I just now see it?" he asks, barely able to think straight.

"Ah, poor baby," Lacey coos, nuzzling his neck. "You can see it now. See?" She does a seductive little shimmy around the room, showing off her long legs, her supple curves, only to laugh when Seth growls and grabs her around the waist, pulling her against him flush.

Lacey whimpers as his hands dig into the flesh of her thighs. But she's smiling. She likes it. His rough grip. They both moan and then Seth's backing her up toward the bed. Tonight, he's taking his time. He's gonna show his girl what she's all about, that he loves her, can't fucking breathe without her.

Any day without Lacey can hurry it the fuck up.

Eyes eager, all she does is watch him. She doesn't have to say what she wants, because Seth knows. Knows the wiggle of her hips, the hitch of her breath that tells him he's doing all the right things.

In a flash, they're on the bed. Seth hovers over her, dipping his mouth to sweep a kiss over her breasts. Lacey's nipples pucker in response to his warm breath, a pleased mewl falling from her lips.

"I ain't ever stoppin', Lacey."

"Stopping what?" She's breathless, her breasts rise.

Off comes her bra, her panties.

"Worshippin' you." The words have her eyes shuttering. "You, Lace, baby." His voice is ragged as he feverishly kisses his way down her svelte body. The slender line of her throat. The jut of her hip bones. The dip of her navel. The warm pulse of her pussy. Lacey moans and arches under his kiss.

When he straightens up, he freezes.

Overcome by emotion, by awe, Seth stares.

The sight of her body, laid out, glowing and gorgeous, damn

near threatens to take him out. He's in awe of this woman who has given everything to him, who's a fighter, a fucking force to be reckoned with.

Sometimes he's still not sure he deserves her. This fucking ocean goddess, this hurricane girl, this woman who's been his savior more times than he can count.

Her body, her breasts, might change, but he cannot imagine anything that would make him want to hold her closer. Because her body is his and he loves it.

Returning to her, his lips skim her jawline. No holding back. All his cards, his love on the table. "You're my favorite person, princess. My favorite scent." With a shiver, she tilts her chin up, meeting his eyes. "You're my ocean. My favorite memory. My favorite *body*." His words hang reverent in the air between them. A sob wrenches from her when he kisses her breasts gently, causing her slender body to wrack. "My wife."

"Your wife," she whispers.

Seth's eyes close, and in that second, between breathless kisses, tangled limbs and hushed *I love you*s, Lacey crying his name, his jeans are unzipped and off. His dick flexes, craving her.

"Mine," he says raggedly, his eyes damp. "You're mine, Lace."

"I am," she gasps, and he thrusts into her. The headboard cracks the wall. "I'm yours."

And then, winding her arms around his neck, Lacey pulls him down to her red lips. He inhales her kiss, drinking her in like water, like sunlight. Lacey loops her legs around his waist drawing him down, deep into her. His hips rear back and then he sinks in deeper. Her heat bathes his cock and Seth groans.

Perfect. She's too damn perfect.

Tears streaming down her face, Lacey buries her face in his neck and kisses him softly. "Forever," she whispers. "We stay like this forever."

"*Yes*," Seth chokes out. Together, their bodies burn, soul to soul, heart to heart in the way they always do. "Till the end of our days, princess. *You*. It's always been you."

# chapter FIFTEEN

SETH BREATHES INTO HIS HANDS.

Paces.

Stops. Checks the time.

Resumes pacing.

Luke runs a hand through his dark hair with a sigh, looking up from his chair. "You wanna get a coffee?"

Seth glowers. "No. I don't want a goddamn coffee."

If his brother thinks he's moving from this spot, he's insane.

"How about a drink?" Griff drawls, a flask appearing in his hands. He passes it to Sal, who takes a pull and passes it to Luke. A soft smile on her face, Alabama shakes her head and takes Griff's hand to still his nerves. Across from them sit Jace and Emmy Lou, an unread magazine draped over the rising swell of Emmy Lou's stomach.

Everyone silent. Stoic. Six people camped out in the family room in solidarity with Seth. Everyone watching the clock tick. Everyone gathered here for him—for Lacey.

It chokes Seth up something fierce.

For his friends and family to be here during one of the worst times in his life means everything to Seth. He's nothing but thankful.

Because he needs them.

Because Lacey's in surgery and he's losing it.

He thought he'd stay calm, steady, but he's a nervous wreck. His head's a mess, and all he can do is replay the memory of this morning. Lacey, in her hospital room, her anxious, beautiful face as she grabbed Seth's shirt and kissed his lips. Tears welled in her eyes. "No goodbyes," she whispered.

Her words gutted him.

He kissed her back, fighting like hell not to break. "No goodbyes."

But now . . .

Now—

Out of Seth comes some unholy strangled sound. "It's been too long."

Sal gives a sympathetic smile. "Only an hour. They said it could take that long."

He smears a hand down his face. Sal's right. Still, the confidence in her voice does nothing to reassure him. Nothing will make him feel better until he sees Lacey.

Lacey needs the surgery, but his girl going under, it's almost more than he can take. There's no way in hell this can go wrong. Absolutely fucking not. Seth reminds himself, it's easy. Routine. He got her the best doctor on the fucking planet. He's researched the procedure and recovery and knows all the risks.

Still . . .

The thought of it going wrong and Lacey not waking up . . . or discovering that her cancer has spread . . .

Christ.

He'd sell his soul to the fucking devil to be with her right now. To make everything okay.

"What did we say? When we were kids?" Seth glances over to see Luke's steady gaze on him. "When we were tryin' to get on those broncs and they kept buckin' us off?"

Seth blinks, getting it.

Seth holds Luke's stare for a moment, then nods. His brother's steady nature is exactly what he needs.

"We said, 'hat low, eyes closed,' and we got back on." Seth exhales a long breath. "We survived. Every damn time."

Luke grins. "That's it."

Jace nods his agreement.

Seth's chest tightens. His band. His brothers. He could never fucking ever do this without them.

Footsteps in the hall.

Seth whips around.

Heads snap up. Sal, her face pale, leans into Luke, who wraps an arm around her shoulders to brace her.

Dr. Mayr approaches, a smile on his face. "How are we doing, folks?" he asks.

*Just fuckin' tell me,* Seth almost shouts at the doctor. That is, he would if his throat could get the words out. But it's stuck. Everything's stuck, like a record and a busted needle, the only thing rattling around in his brain is Lacey.

*Lacey.*

*Lacey.*

His heartbeat.

His hurricane.

His everything.

The only thing keeping him steady right now.

"How is she?" he finally manages to get out. "How's my wife?"

"Everything went beautifully."

Seth closes his eyes. Thank God. *Thank God.*

The entire waiting room unclenches. Sal laughs and Luke wraps her up in a big hug. Emmy Lou bursts into tears, her belly bobbing with her sobs, Jace dipping his head to talk to her in a reassuring voice. Griff and Alabama's wild whoops fill the air.

Pulling Seth aside, Mayr speaks to him privately. "We were able to remove the tissue and preserve as much of the natural breast as possible. We'll send the tissue to pathology to determine the final size of the tumor and whether or not there are clear margins, but I'm anticipating good news."

Seth nods, an unexpected lightness filling his chest as he takes in the doctor's words.

Mayr continues. "Your wife's been moved to the recovery room. We'll monitor her vitals for a few hours and then she can recover at home." He smiles. "When she's awake, we'll discuss next steps, but right now, you can see her."

Seth shakes the guy's hand. His heart feels like it wants to punch a hole in his chest. "Thank you. Thank you so damn much."

It's the chirp of monitors that wakes her first.

And then the death grip on her right hand.

Slowly, Lacey blinks herself awake. Back to the present. Back to her husband's handsome face staring down at her.

Seth, sitting on the edge of her bed, lets out a ragged, relieved breath. "Hey, princess." Gently, her hand's brought to his lips as he sweeps a kiss across her knuckles. His intent gaze searches her face. "How you feelin'?"

"Mmm." Lacey's lips lift in a half-smile. "Stoned."

She lies still, taking in her body. She feels dreamy, but her body aches. There's a tightness in her chest, a strange numbness in her left arm near the armpit.

Lacey's curious eyes take in the room. Already, gorgeous bouquets of flowers fill the room. Cheery Get Well Soon cards line the windowsill.

Then, she looks at Seth. Takes in the worry dancing in his ocean-blue eyes. "How are you?" she whispers.

"Better now that you're awake." He squeezes her hand. "I was shakin' in my boots out there, Lace. Everyone was."

"Everyone?"

He grins. "Everyone came. Waitin' on word."

Lacey's eyes widen. Her lower lip trembles. Hot moisture at the backs of her eyes at the thought of her friends being there to support Seth. "Oh. Oh wow."

Seth smiles, his eyes damp. "You did good, princess. The doc said everything went great with your surgery." His voice trembles with emotion and a shaky exhale rumbles out of him. "Christ.

You've been so fuckin' brave. So strong." His hand palms the crown of her head. "I'm so goddamn proud of you."

Lacey lets out a long sigh. The warmth of his words, his love inked on her heart.

Seth leans down, brushing a kiss to her mouth. She grips his arm, a slow heat wave in her belly. All she wants to do is get out of this hospital, away from the beeps of the machines and be with Seth.

"Lay with me," she says.

His face softening, he gives a nod of assent, and then he's carefully swinging himself up beside her, boots and all, his long, lean body cradling hers protectively.

They lie together in the bed, a sync of hearts, of breaths. Seth traces his fingers up her arm and she fights a shiver. Fights the urge to climb on top of him. She already knows Seth would put a very unfair stop to that.

So she settles for snuggling into him, inhaling his heady scent. Then, taking in the crystal blue of his eyes, Lacey says, "Remember that time I thought this year would be all about my career and wedding? Wow, was I off. Like way, way off."

Seth laughs and lays his mouth against her ear. "Now it ain't that bad."

"Oh, it isn't?"

"You still got a handsome husband to call your own."

She hums consideringly.

"When can I get out of here?" she asks.

He groans. "You ain't gonna give me a minute to relax, are you?"

She smiles. "Never."

His grin fades into a serious expression. "Soon. The doctor will be back to talk to you, you'll rest here for a few hours, then I take you home."

She closes her eyes. *Home.*

She can't wait.

"Just know," Seth says, and she opens her eyes. His mouth is twitching, humor in his gaze, "I'm ready. Ready to change bandages. Ready to boss you around."

She scoffs, puts a hand to her forehead. "A honeymoon in bed. How very unglamorous."

Seth gives her a stern look. "Put the pout away, princess. You're stayin' in that bed until I personally discharge you. Two weeks. Out of commission."

She groans. "You're a sadist."

"Hell, you ain't gonna be alone."

She arches a brow. "Oh no?"

"Hell no." Seth captures her mouth in one long, sweet kiss. "It's gonna be the best kind of honeymoon. Horror movies. Pizza. A gorgeous green-eyed blond listening to her handsome husband's wise words of wisdom while she heals."

Lacey laughs.

Seth tugs her close. "You hear that, princess? We're stayin' in bed all day."

She smiles. "Could be a good thing."

Seth kisses her as he tightens his arms around her. "Could be a great thing."

# epilogue

*Six Months Later*

All across the country land, October sunshine.

The click-clack of Lacey's heels sounds out over the concrete slab foundation. She glances down at the strewn tools and dust, glances up into the high beams of the house. The frame's taking shape. She can practically picture her modern farmhouse. Bright white. Black trimmed windows. Views that go on for days.

A sound has her turning. Seth's Bronco lurches into a spot beside her car. Out comes Seth, disheveled hair, plaid shirt rolled to his elbows, dusty boots, blue jeans.

"You're late," she says, arching a brow at her husband.

"Shit," he says, slapping hands against the thighs of his jeans as he hops up onto the foundation. "Takin' after you."

She scoffs. "I'm never late."

"Please. If it weren't for me, we'd miss ninety percent of our flights."

She sticks out her tongue at him, laughing now. Then she walks right into his outstretched arms. Seth rocks her in a hug and Lacey lets out a happy sigh. She's ached for this all day. Seth's touch. His tight squeeze. His steadying strength.

He pulls back and cups her face. "What do you think of the house?"

She tosses her hair and smiles. "It's coming together."

Just like Lacey.

Since her surgery, her life's fallen into a sort of chaotic order.

Her pathology results came back with good news—clear margins, which means her cancer didn't spread. Five times a week for five weeks she did radiation. The treatment left her tired and nauseous, but everyone pitched in to help. Friends and family brought meals and helped with the housework; even Griff Greyson shuttled her to an appointment when Seth couldn't break a gig. Now her cocktail for the next three years is Tamoxifen. The drug makes her tired and dizzy at times, but she's learning to live with it. It'll be three full years before she can end the treatment, but until then Lacey's content.

She's blessed to have such diligent friends and good doctors.

She's learned so much the last six months.

Most importantly, how to cast aside fear and focus on what's in front of her.

To just be *here*, with Seth, it's more than she can ever hope for.

It's all she wants.

Smiling at her husband, she goes on, "Do you know what's right above us?"

"Heaven?" he drawls.

She rolls her eyes. "No, Seth. The master bedroom. More importantly . . . the master bath."

He steps closer, running his hands down her arm. "You know, I'm goin' to miss sharin' a bathroom with you."

"Liar."

He laughs, roving his eyes around the massive space. "Already plannin' the housewarming party, princess?"

She palms his chest. "You know it." She kisses him, then ruffles his messy shock of sandy-blond hair. "How was practice?" For the last week, the Brothers Kincaid have been busy laying down tracks for their much-anticipated new album *Out and Down*. And soon, a tour.

"We burned it up today. Nashville ain't gonna know what hit 'em."

Lacey smiles, awe burning a hole in her chest. She's so proud of the Brothers Kincaid. She thought she knew what went into a song, an album, only she didn't realize the half of it. Seth and his boys work nonstop, and she already knows their tenth album is going to be record-breaking.

Seth slides his fingers through hers and squeezes, pulling her into him. Love flashes in his eyes. "How 'bout you? You okay today?"

*Okay today.*

Their reminder to each other to take it one day at a time. To live in the present because life is short.

Lacey leans into him, nestling into his broad chest, his warmth. "A little tired. But good."

His arm cleaving her tighter against him, Seth watches her close, his ocean-blue eyes taking her in. Clocking her, checking on her, worrying about her, and for that she loves him.

So damn much.

Lacey will never stop being grateful for this man. Because Seth's there. He always has been and he always will be.

The way he's showed up for her these last six months. Cancelling gigs, rescheduling tours, being with her at every appointment even if she insisted that she was fine. Watching her like a hawk to make sure she didn't overexert or overextend herself.

With everything that's happened the last year, she never expected cancer, but she's better for it. She loves harder. Fights stronger. Having a supportive, loving partner who gives her strength and hope made such a difference in her recovery and treatment.

Seth's rumble of a chuckle takes her from her thoughts. "Looks like the party's already gettin' started."

Uncurling from his arms, Lacey follows Seth's gaze.

Off in the distance, Wild Antler Farm. Griff's jacked-up GMC sits in the drive. It's the last time they'll see their friends for a while. Recently making history as the only married country couple to have four songs in the Top Ten on country radio, Griff and Alabama are off to Europe for a month-long tour that sold out in five minutes.

Dust trails kick up, signaling the arrival of Emmy Lou, Jace and their twins, Cora and Daisy. The babies who were born in June, are the newest and cutest addition to their country music family.

Seth gives her a close look. "You still feel up for goin' to Sunday supper?"

Lacey angles her head. "Uh, yes, please. And miss Sal's announcement? Never."

"What do you think it is?" Mischief stains Seth's voice.

Lacey narrows her eyes. At the hoodwink in his expression, she gasps and slaps a hand against his chest. "Do you know?"

"Do *you* know?"

"*Seth.*"

"*Lacey.*"

Vehemently, Lacey shakes her head, rallying every ounce of willpower not to spill the beans. "Sal will kill me if I tell you. She'll just know. She's all-knowing like that."

Seth gives a lazy shrug and wraps an arm around her waist. "I reckon we'll have to see tonight."

They stand there, watching the sunset, and then, unable to help herself, Lacey side-eyes him, says, "It's a girl."

Seth laughs, bright and joyful. "Bet you, princess, it's a boy."

She scoffs. "Never."

Seth pulls her into his arms, bracing Lacey up against his broad chest, and they turn toward the countryside, drinking in the views, the October sunshine. They're quiet for a long time, Seth holding her to him, his grip tight and steady. The sweetgrass sways, a red-tailed hawk skirts the horizon. Happiness and love are a graceful wave inside of her. Lacey looks up at the sky. A tapestry of colors, of beauty, of hope.

And in that second, that beautiful, glorious second, Lacey sees it all.

Their future.

Sunday suppers, their own traditions like poker night and horror movie Fridays, lazy mornings with Seth bickering, always bickering over their shared bathroom space, and down the line, maybe babies, but it's not a sure thing, and she and Seth are okay with that. They have each other and that's enough. All she needs to get by in this whirlwind she calls a life.

She and Seth—they'll keep doing what they're doing, living their lives, just keep on writing their love song.

One day at a time.

And then, the sweetest whisper in her ear. "I love you, Lace."

She twists in his arms to face Seth, staring up at his handsome face. Her eyes fill with unshed tears when he presses a gentle kiss to her forehead.

"I love you," she says breathlessly.

Seth strokes a finger across her cheek. "Better days," he says, his voice choked by emotion. "We got 'em, princess. Right here. Right now."

Lacey smiles. "With you."

## *books by*
# AVA HUNTER

**The Nashville Star Series**

*Know You More – a Prequel*

*Sing You Home*

*Find You Again*

*Love You Always – a Novella*

*Need You Now*

*Bring You Back*

*With You Forever – a Novella*

# acknowledgments

This novella is a little work of love. Seth and Lacey had a bit more story to tell and I really hope I did them, and this topic, justice.

Thank you to everyone who has read and loved the Nashville Star series. I appreciate you so, so much.

Thank you to Mel for reading this before anyone else.

Thank you to my old standby: the trauma fiction group on Facebook. Another time you've come through with your medical advice, knowledge and experience.

Thanks to my family.

# about the AUTHOR

Ava Hunter is a strong believer in black coffee, red wine, and the there's-only-one-bed trope. She writes contemporary romance with healthy amounts of angst, where the damsels are never quite damsels, but the men they love (good, bad and rugged) are always there for them. Her first series, Nashville Star, centers on sexy country singers and their honky-tonk drama-filled lives. She writes from her home in Arizona, where she lives with her husband and daughter.

Don't miss out on Ava Hunter's upcoming books!
Subscribe to her newsletter:
www.authoravahunter.com

www.ingramcontent.com/pod-product-compliance
Lightning Source LLC
Chambersburg PA
CBHW011043190726
48290CB00011B/2971
* 9 7 8 1 7 3 7 4 7 4 3 5 7 *